To The Samurai—

If you're all reading this, it means you survived your month here at the lodge. I bet you thought it was going to drive you crazy, right? None of us were ever the type to settle down for long. That's why I made those twenty million dollars dependent on your sticking around. Money talks, bros. I'm glad you all made it.

Meri always said I was the guy who kept you all together, and she was afraid that after I was gone, The Samurai would be no more. Well, I wasn't about to let that happen. When I got sick I discovered what really mattered. Have *you* figured it out yet?

Yeah, I thought so.

Hunter

Dear Reader,

I've always believed that friends are the family we make.
That belief carries over to my writing, where I tell stories
about friends.

The MILLIONAIRE OF THE MONTH series has been
about friends. In my book, Jack and Meredith once were
good friends. Then time and distance got in the way.
Meri thinks she's back to get closure and maybe a little
revenge, but she's wrong. She's back because she's still
in love with her friend.

In Bed with the Devil wraps up the series, but don't
worry if you've missed the other books. I wrote it to
stand alone. However, if you've become a fan of the
series, you'll enjoy catching up with all the previous
characters. And meeting Hunter...

One of the coolest parts about being a romance writer
is meeting other writers. These women are intelligent,
caring and incredibly funny—qualities I want in my
friends. It was a pleasure to work with them.

Happy reading,

Susan Mallery

IN BED WITH
THE DEVIL

SUSAN
MALLERY

Silhouette® Desire

Published by Silhouette Books

America's Publisher of Contemporary Romance

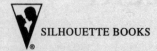

SILHOUETTE BOOKS

ISBN-13: 978-0-373-76815-8
ISBN-10:   0-373-76815-X

IN BED WITH THE DEVIL

Copyright © 2007 by Susan Macias Redmond

All rights reserved. Except for use in any review, the reproduction or utilization of this work in whole or in part in any form by any electronic, mechanical or other means, now known or hereafter invented, including xerography, photocopying and recording, or in any information storage or retrieval system, is forbidden without the written permission of the editorial office, Silhouette Books, 233 Broadway, New York, NY 10279 U.S.A.

This is a work of fiction. Names, characters, places and incidents are either the product of the author's imagination or are used fictitiously, and any resemblance to actual persons, living or dead, business establishments, events or locales is entirely coincidental.

This edition published by arrangement with Harlequin Books S.A.

® and TM are trademarks of Harlequin Books S.A., used under license. Trademarks indicated with ® are registered in the United States Patent and Trademark Office, the Canadian Trade Marks Office and in other countries.

Visit Silhouette Books at www.eHarlequin.com

Printed in U.S.A.

SUSAN MALLERY

is a bestselling and award-winning author of over fifty books for Harlequin Books and Silhouette Books. She makes her home in the Los Angeles area with her handsome prince of a husband and her two adorable-but-not-bright cats.

To the fabulously talented authors in this series.
Thank you so much for inviting me along for the ride. It
was wonderful fun and I would do it again in a heartbeat!

One

Eleven years ago...

Meredith Palmer spent the afternoon of her seventeenth birthday curled up on her narrow bed, sobbing uncontrollably. Everything about her life was a disaster. It was never going to be better—and what if she was one of the unlucky people who peaked in her teenage years? What if this was the *best* it was going to be?

Seriously, she should just throw herself out her dorm room window and be done with it. Of course, she was only on the fourth floor, so she was not going to actually kill herself. The most likely event was maiming.

She sat up and wiped her face. "Given the distance to the ground and the speed at impact," she murmured

to herself, then sniffed. "Depending on my position…"
She reached for a piece of paper. "If I fell feet first—
unlikely, but it could happen—then the majority of the
stress would be on my…"

She started doing the calculations. Bone density
versus a hard concrete landing or a softer grass landing.
Assuming a coefficient of—

Meri threw down the pencil and paper and collapsed
back on her bed. "I'm a total freak. I'll never be anything
but a freak. I should be planning my *death*, not doing
math. No wonder I don't have any friends."

The sobs returned. She cried and cried, knowing that
there was no cure for her freakishness. That she was
destined to be one of those scary solitary people.

"I'll have to get cats," she cried. "I'm allergic to cats."

The door to her room opened. She kept her face
firmly in her pillow.

"Go away."

"I don't think so."

That voice. She knew that voice. The owner was the
star of every romantic and semisexual fantasy she'd
ever had. Tall, with dark hair and eyes the color of the
midnight sky—assuming one was away from the city,
where the ambient light emitted enough of a—

Meri groaned. "Someone just kill me now."

"No one's going to kill you," Jack said as he sat
next to her on her bed and put a strong, large hand on
her back. "Come on, kid. It's your birthday. What's
the problem?"

How much time did he have? She could make him a
list. Given an extra forty-five seconds, she could index

it, translate it into a couple of languages, then turn it into computer code.

"I hate my life. It's horrible. I'm a freak. Worse, I'm a fat, ugly freak and I'll always be this way."

She heard Jack draw in a breath.

There were a lot of reasons she was totally in love with him. Sure, he was incredibly good-looking, but that almost didn't matter. The best part of Jack was he took time with her. He talked to her as if she was a real person. Next to Hunter, her brother, she loved Jack more than anyone.

"You're not a freak," he said, his voice low.

She noticed he didn't say she wasn't fat. There was no getting around the extra forty pounds on her five-foot-two-inch, small-boned frame. Unfortunately he also didn't tell her she wasn't ugly. Jack was kind, but he wasn't a liar.

Between her braces and her nose—which rivaled the size of Io, one of Jupiter's moons—and her blotchy complexion, she had a permanent offer from the circus to sign on up for the sideshow.

"I'm not normal," she said, still speaking into her pillow because crying made her puffy and she didn't need for Jack to see her looking even *more* hideous. "I was planning my death and instead I got caught up in math equations. Normal people don't do that."

"You're right, Meri. You're not normal. You're way better than that. You're a genius. The rest of us are idiots."

He wasn't an idiot. He was perfect.

"I've been in college since I was twelve," she mumbled. "That's five years. If I was really smart, I'd be done now."

"You're getting a Ph.D., not to mention your, what, third masters?"

"Something like that." Unable to be in the same room with him and not look at him, she flipped onto her back.

God, he was so amazing, she thought as her chest tightened and her stomach turned over a couple of times. Technically the organ in question couldn't turn over. What she felt was just—

She covered her face with her hands. "I have to find a way to turn off my brain."

"Why? So you can be like the rest of us?"

She dropped her hands to her side. "Yes. I want to be a regular girl."

"Sorry. You're stuck being special."

She loved him so much it hurt. She wanted him to think she was more than his best friend's kid sister. She wanted him to see her as a woman.

Right, and while she was having a fantasy moment…

maybe he could see her as a beautiful woman he ached for. As if!

"I don't have any friends," she said as she did her best to ignore the need to tell him she would love him forever. "I'm too young, especially in the Ph.D. program. They all think I'm some upstart kid. They're waiting for me to crash and burn."

"Which isn't going to happen."

"I know, but between my academic isolation and my lack of a female role model since the death of my mother, the odds of my maturing to a normal functioning member of society grow more slim each day. Like I said—I'm a freak." Tears rolled down her temples to get lost in her hair. "I'll never have a boyfriend."

"Give it a couple of years."

"It's not going to happen. And even if some guy does take pity on me and ask me out, he'll have to be drunk or stoned or something to want to kiss me, let alone have sex with me. I'm going to d-die a virgin."

The sobs began again.

Jack pulled her into a sitting position and wrapped his arms around her. "Hell of a birthday," he said.

"Tell me about it."

She snuggled close, liking how strong and muscular he felt. He smelled good, too. If only he were desperately in love with her, the moment would be perfect.

But that was not meant to be. Instead of declaring undying devotion and ripping off both their clothes or even kissing her, he shifted back so they weren't even touching.

"Meri, you're in a tough place right now. You don't fit in here and you sure don't fit in with kids your own age."

She wanted to protest she was almost his age—there were only four years between them—and she fit with him just fine. But Jack was the kind of guy who had dozens of women lining up to be with him. Pretty, skinny girls she really, really hated.

"But you're going to get through this and then life is going to be a whole lot better."

"I don't think so. Freakishness doesn't just go away."

He reached out and touched her cheek. "I have high hopes for you."

"What if you're wrong? What if I do die a virgin?"

He chuckled. "You won't. I promise."

"Cheap talk."

"It's what I'm good at."

He leaned toward her, and before she knew what he was going to do, he kissed her. On the mouth!

She barely registered the soft, warm pressure of his lips on hers and then the kiss was over.

"No!" She spoke without thinking and grabbed the front of his sweatshirt. "Jack, no. Please. I want you to be my first time."

She'd never seen a man move so fast. One second he was on her bed, the next he was standing by the door to her dorm room.

Shame and humiliation swept through her. She would have given a hundred IQ points to call those words back. Heat burned her cheeks until she knew she would be marked by the embarrassment forever.

She'd never meant him to know. He'd probably guessed she had a massive crush on him, but she'd never wanted him to be sure.

"Jack, I…"

He shook his head. "Meri, I'm sorry. You're…you're Hunter's little sister. I could never… I don't see you like that."

Of course not. Why would he want a beast when there were so many beauties throwing themselves at him?

"I understand. Everything. Just go."

He started to leave, then turned back. "I want us to be friends. You're my friend, Meri." And with those horrifying words, he left.

Meri sat on the edge of her bed and wondered when she would stop hurting so much. When would she fit in?

When would she stop loving Jack? When would she be able to walk in a room and not wish for the floor to open up and swallow her whole?

Automatically she reached under her bed and pulled out the plastic storage container filled with her snacks. After grabbing a frosted cupcake, she unwrapped it.

This was it—she'd officially hit bottom. Nothing would ever be worse than this exact moment. It was like dark matter in the universe. The absolute absence of anything. It was the death of hope.

She took a bite of the cupcake. Shame made her chew fast and swallow. When the sugar and fat hit her system, she wouldn't hurt so bad. She wouldn't feel so lonely or totally rejected by Jack Howington III. Damn him.

Why couldn't he love her back? She was a good person. But she wasn't busty and blond and tiny, like the girls he dated and slept with.

"I have a brain," she murmured. "That scares guys."

She said the words bravely, but she knew it was more than her incredible IQ that chased off boys. It was how she looked. How she'd allowed food to be everything, especially after her mom died four years ago. It was turning down her father's badly worded offer to take her to a plastic surgeon to talk about her nose. She screamed that if he really loved her, he would never, ever talk about it again, when in truth she was scared. Scared of changing and scared of being the same.

She stood and stared at the closed dorm room door. "I hate you, Jack," she said as tears slipped down her cheeks. "I hate you and I'll make you suffer. I'm going to grow up and be so beautiful you have to sleep with me. Then I'm going to walk away and break your heart. Just watch me."

Present day

Jack Howington III had driven two days straight to get to Lake Tahoe. He could have flown his jet, then picked up a rental car for the month he was going to be forced to stay at Hunter's house, but he'd needed the downtime to clear his head.

His assistant had been frantic, unable to reach him in the more rural parts of the country, but he'd enjoyed the silence. There hadn't been enough silence in his life for a long, long time. Even when he was alone, there were still the damn ghosts to contend with.

He drove down a long driveway toward a barely visible log house. The place stood surrounded by trees with a view of the lake behind. There were windows and stone steps, along with a heavy double wood door.

Jack parked, then climbed out of his Mercedes. Hunter's house had been built just recently, nearly ten years after the death of his friend, but Jack had a feeling that Hunter had left detailed instructions on what it should look like. The place reminded him of Hunter, which was both good and bad.

It was just a month, he told himself as he walked around to the trunk and grabbed his suitcase and computer bag. If he stayed in here for a month, per the terms of Hunter's will, the house would be converted to a place for cancer patients and survivors to come for free. Twenty million would be given to the town or charity or something like that. Jack hadn't paid attention to the details. All he knew was that Hunter had asked him for one last favor. Jack had failed his friend enough times to know that this time he had to follow through.

He took a single step toward the house, then stopped as the front door opened. The lawyer's letter had promised quiet, an office he could work in and a housekeeper to take care of day-to-day necessities.

Easy duty, Jack had thought at the time. Now, as a petite, pretty woman stepped onto the porch, he wasn't so sure.

Next to Hunter, who was long dead, she was about the last person he wanted to see.

"Hello, Jack," she said.

"Meredith."

Her blue eyes widened in surprise. "You recognize me?"

"Sure. Why not?"

She drew in a breath. "It's been a long time. We've both changed."

"I'd know you anywhere."

Which wasn't exactly the truth. He'd kept tabs on Meri over the years. It was the least he could do after he'd promised Hunter he would look after his sister. Jack hadn't been able to deal with her in person, but distance made things safer. Easier. The regular reports from his staff meant he wasn't the least bit surprised by her appearance. Although she looked more…feminine than usual. He'd known she'd been working in California on a temporary assignment with JPL—Jet Propulsion Laboratory, but not the details. He hadn't known she was *here*.

She muttered something under her breath, then said, "Good to know."

Her eyes were still as blue as he remembered. The same color as Hunter's eyes. The same shape. Other than that and an easy laugh, the siblings had had little in common.

He hadn't seen her in years. Not since Hunter's funeral. And before that—

He pushed the memory of her heartfelt declaration and his piss-poor handling of it out of his mind. Let's just say they'd both traveled a lot of years and miles, he told himself.

She'd grown up, he thought as she walked down the stairs and stood in front of him. The baby fat was gone. She looked like what she was—a beautiful, sexy woman who was confident of her place in the world.

Under other circumstances, he could have appreciated the changes, but not with her. Not with the promises he'd made.

"Obviously you received the letter from the lawyer or you wouldn't be here," she said. "You're required to stay for a month. At the end of that time, there will be a brief but meaningful ceremony deeding the house to the town, handing over the keys and the money. You and the other Samurai are free to mingle and catch up, then you're free to go." She glanced at the single suitcase and computer bag. "You travel light."

"Makes it easier to move around."

"But it doesn't give you many choices for that unexpected costume party."

"Is there going to be one?"

"Not that I know of."

"Then I'm good."

She tilted her head slightly, a gesture he remembered. Funny how he could still see the girl in the woman. He'd always liked the girl. He didn't plan to get to know the woman.

He looked her over, then frowned. Was it just him or were her shorts way too short? Not that he didn't appreciate the display of leg, but this was Meredith—Hunter's baby sister. And should her shirt really be that…revealing?

"I'm staying here, too."

Her voice was low and sexy, and had she been anyone else, he would have welcomed the distraction.

"Why?" he asked bluntly.

"I'm the housekeeper. The one you were promised. I'm here to make your life…easier."

There was almost a challenge in the statement. "I don't need a housekeeper."

"You're not being given a choice. I come with the property."

"That's ridiculous," he said flatly. He happened to know she worked for a D.C. think tank and was currently on loan to JPL and some private company, helping them develop a better solid rocket fuel.

"Such language," she scolded gently, then smiled. "It's what Hunter wanted. We're both here because of him."

He frowned. He didn't buy her story. Why would Hunter want his sister at the house for a month? But then, he'd asked all his friends to spend time here, so it was possible. Besides, it wasn't as if Meri would *want* to be in the same house as him. Not after what had happened on her seventeenth birthday.

He'd hurt her. He hadn't meant to, but he had, and after the fact he'd been unable to figure out a way to make things better. Then Hunter had died and everything had changed.

Or maybe he was making too big a deal out of all this. Maybe Meri didn't give a damn about what had happened…or not happened…between them.

"Let's go inside," she said and led the way.

They walked into a large entryway with a staircase and a stone floor. The place was welcoming and masculine. It might not be the house he would have built, but it wasn't going to drive him crazy with lots of frills and smelly bowls of dried flowers.

"You'll get your exercise climbing the stairs. Your room is on the next floor."

He glanced around. "You're down here?"

She smiled. "No, Jack. I'm on the second floor, next to the master. We're only a wall apart."

Meri deliberately widened her eyes and leaned toward him as she spoke. She wanted the invitation to be clear. After what Jack had put her through eleven years ago, he deserved to squirm.

She started down the hall before he had a chance to respond. "There's an office loft area," she continued. "You can use that. It's set up with Internet access, a fax. I'll be in the dining room. I like to spread out when I work. I tend to get really…involved."

She emphasized the last word, then had to consciously keep herself from laughing. Okay, this was way more fun than she'd thought it would be. She should have punished Jack a long time ago.

She made sure she swayed her hips as she climbed and bent forward slightly so he would be sure to notice her very short shorts. She'd worn them deliberately, along with the halter top that left very little to the imagination. It had taken her nearly two days to come up with the perfect outfit, but it had been worth the time.

The shorts clung to her and were cut high enough to show the bottom of her butt. Tacky but effective. Her sandals had a spiked heel that was practically a weapon, but they made her legs look long—a serious trick for someone as short as her.

The halter was so low-cut that she'd had to hold it in place with double-sided tape. She had fresh highlights, sultry makeup and long, dangling earrings that almost touched her nearly bare shoulders.

If the guys back at her science lab could see her now, they would probably implode from shock. Around them she only wore tailored suits and lab jackets. But for the next month she was dressing as a sex kitten and she planned to enjoy every minute of it.

She deliberately sped up at the end of the hall, then stopped suddenly. Jack ran into her. He reached out to steady himself or maybe her. She'd planned that he would, so she turned and held in a grin as the palm of his hand landed exactly on her left breast.

He stiffened and pulled back so fast he almost fell. Meri tried to decide if she minded seeing him in a crumpled heap on the polished hardwood floor.

"Sorry," he muttered.

"Jack," she purred. "Are you coming on to me? I have to say, that's not very subtle. I would have expected better."

"I'm not coming on to you."

"Really?" She put her hands on her hips as she faced him. "Why not? Aren't I your type?"

He frowned. "What the hell is this all about?"

"So many things. I'm not sure where to start."

"Try at the beginning. It usually works for me."

The beginning? Where was that? At conception, where some quirk of the Palmer gene pool had decided to produce a child with an exceptional IQ? Or later, when Meri had first realized she was never going to fit in anywhere? Or perhaps that long-ago-but-never-forgotten-afternoon when the man she loved had so cruelly rejected her?

"We're spending the month together," she told him. "I thought we could have more fun if we played. I know you like to play, Jack."

He swore under his breath. "This isn't like you, Meri."

"How can you be sure? It's been a long time. I've grown up." She turned slowly. "Don't you like the changes?"

"You look great. You know that. So what's the point?"

The point was she wanted him desperate. She wanted him panting, begging, pleading. Then she would give in and walk away. It was her plan—it had always been her plan.

"I'm not going to sleep with you," he said flatly. "You're Hunter's sister. I gave him my word I'd look after you. That means taking care of you, not sleeping with you."

She'd meant to keep her temper. Honestly she'd even written it on her to-do list. But it was simply impossible.

"Take care of me? Is that what you call disappearing two seconds after Hunter's funeral? All of you left—all of his friends. I expected it of them but not of you. Hunter told me you would always be there for me no matter what. But you weren't. You were gone. I was seventeen, Jack. My father was a basket case, I was a total social outcast with no friends and you disappeared. Because that was easier than facing your responsibility."

He put down his luggage. "Is that why you're here? To tell me off?"

He had no idea, she thought, still furious and wishing she could breathe fire and burn him into a little stick figure, like in the cartoons.

"That's only part of the fun."

"Would it help if I said I was sorry?"

"No, it wouldn't." Nothing would change the fact that he'd abandoned her, just like everyone else she'd ever loved.

"Meri, I know we have some history. But if we're stuck here for a month, we need to find a way to get along."

"Be friends, you mean?" she said, remembering how he'd said he would always be her friend, right after rejecting her.

"If you'd like."

She took a deep breath, then released it. "No, Jack. We'll never be friends. We'll be lovers and nothing else."

Two

The next morning Meri woke up feeling much better about everything. After leaving out food for Jack, she'd escaped to her room, where she'd had a bath and a good cry. Some of her tears had been about her brother, but a lot of them had been for herself. For the geek she'd been and the losses she'd suffered.

After Hunter had died, their father had totally lost it. He'd been less than useless to her. Within a year he'd started dating nineteen-year-olds, and in the nine years since, his girlfriends had stayed depressingly young.

She'd been on her own and she'd survived. Wasn't that what mattered? That she'd managed to get the help she'd needed to move forward and thrive?

She turned on her clock's radio and rocked her hips to the disco music that blasted into the room. She was sorry she'd missed the disco years—the music had such a driving beat. Of course, she was a total spaz on the dance floor, but what she lacked in style and grace she made up for in enthusiasm.

After brushing out her hair, she braided it, then dressed in a sports bra, tank top and another pair of skimpy shorts. Ankle socks and athletic shoes completed her outfit.

Humming "We Are Family" under her breath, she left her room and prepared to implement the next part of her plan for revenge.

Jack was in the kitchen. She walked up to him and smiled.

"Morning," she said, reaching past him for the pot of coffee. She made sure she leaned against him rather than going around. "How did you sleep?"

His dark eyes flickered slightly, but his expression never changed. "Fine."

"Good. Me, too."

She poured the coffee, then took a sip, looking at him over the mug.

"So," she said. "A whole month. That's a long time. Whatever will we do with it?"

"Not what you have planned."

She allowed herself a slight smile. "I remember you saying that before. Did you always repeat yourself? I remember you being a whole lot more articulate. Of course, I was younger then, and one looks at one's elders with the idealism of youth."

He nearly choked on his coffee. "Elders?"

"Time has been passing, Jack. You're, what, nearly forty?"

"I'm thirty-two and you know it."

"Oh, right. Thirty-two. Time has been a challenge for you, hasn't it?"

She enjoyed baiting him too much, she thought, knowing she was being totally evil and unable to help herself. The truth was, Jack looked amazing. Fit, sexy—a man in his prime. The good news was that sleeping with him wouldn't be a hardship.

"You gave up on seducing me?" he asked.

"Not at all. But this is fun, too."

"I'm not sleeping with you."

She glanced around the kitchen, then looked back at him. "I'm sorry, did you say something? I wasn't listening."

"You're a pain in the ass."

"But it's a darned nice ass, isn't it?" She turned to show him, patted the curve, then faced front again. "Okay, go get changed. I'll take you to the nearest gym. You can get a thirty-day membership. Then we'll work out together."

"There's no equipment here?"

She smiled. "I guess Hunter didn't think of everything after all. It's a good thing I'm around."

He stared at her. "You think you're in charge?"

"Uh-huh."

He put down his mug, then moved close and stared into her eyes. "Be careful, Meri. You're playing a game you don't know how to win. I'm out of your league and we both know it."

A challenge? Was he crazy? She always won and she would this time. Although there was something about the way he looked at her that made her shiver. Something that told her he was not a man to be toyed with.

But he *was* just a man, she reminded herself. The sooner she got him into bed, the quicker she could get on with her life.

Jack followed Meri into the large gym overlooking the lake. The facility was light and clean, with only a few people working out. Probably because it was midday, he thought as he took in the new equipment and mentally planned his workout.

Back in Dallas, he worked out in his private gym, built to his specifications. But this would do for now.

"So we can circuit-train together," she said brightly, standing close and gazing up at him with a teasing smile. "I'm great at spotting."

She was trying to push his buttons. He was determined not to react, regardless of what she said or did. Meri was playing a game that could be dangerous to her. He might not have taken care of her the way he should have, but he *had* looked out for her. That wasn't going to stop just because she was determined to prove a point.

"Want to warm up with some cardio first?" she asked. "We can race. I'll even give you a head start."

"I'm not going to need it," he told her as he headed over to the treadmills, not bothering to see if she followed.

"That's what you think."

She stepped onto the machine next to his and set it for a brisk warm-up pace. He did the same, not bothering to look at her speed.

"You didn't used to exercise," he said conversation-ally a few minutes later as he broke into a jog.

Meri punched a few buttons on her treadmill and matched his speed. "I know. I was much more into food than anything else. Not surprising—food was my only friend."

"We were friends," he said before he could stop himself. He'd liked Meri—she was Hunter's little sister. She'd been like family to him.

"Food was the only friend I could depend on," she said as she cranked up her treadmill again. She was breathing a little harder but barely breaking a sweat. "It didn't disappear when I needed it most."

No point in defending himself. She was right—he'd taken off right after Hunter's funeral. He'd been too dev-astated by loss and guilt to stick around. A few months later he'd realized he needed to make sure Meri was all right. So he'd hired a P.I. to check in on her every few months. The quarterly reports had given him the basics about her life but nothing specific. Later, when he'd started his own company, he'd gotten his people to keep tabs on her and he'd learned a lot more about her. He'd learned that she'd grown up into a hell of a woman. Obviously she hadn't needed him around, taking care of things.

"The downside of food as a friend," she continued, "is that there's an ugly side effect. Still, I couldn't seem to stop eating. Then one day I made some new friends and I stopped needing the food so much." She grinned. "Okay, friends and some serious therapy."

"You were in therapy?" The reports hadn't mentioned that.

"For a couple of years. I worked through my issues. I'm too smart and weird to ever be completely normal, but these days I know how to pass."

"You're not weird," he said, knowing better than to challenge her brain. Meri had always been on the high side of brilliant.

"A lot you know," she said. "But I like who I am now. I accept the good points and the bad."

There were plenty of good points, he thought, doing his best not to look at her trim body. She had plenty of curves, all in the right places.

They continued to jog next to each other. After another five minutes, Meri increased the speed again and went into a full-out run. Jack's competitive side kicked in. He increased not only the speed but the incline.

"You think you're so tough," she muttered, her breath coming fast and hard now.

"You'll never win this battle," he told her. "I have long legs and more muscle mass."

"That just means more weight to haul around."

She ran a couple more minutes, then hit the stop button and straddled the tread. After wiping her face and gulping water, she went back onto the treadmill but at a much slower pace. He ran a few more minutes—because he could—then started his cooldown.

"You're in shape," he told her as they walked over to the weight room.

"I know." She smiled. "I'm a wild woman with the free weights. This is where you really get to show off, what with having more upper-body strength. But pound for pound, I'm actually lifting nearly as much as you. Want me to make a graph?"

He grinned. "No, thanks. I can see your excuses without visual aids."

"Reality is never an excuse," she told him as she collected several weights, then walked over to a bench. She wiped her hands on the towel she'd brought.

"I can't be too sweaty," she said. "If my hands are slick, it gets dangerous. About a year ago, I nearly dropped a weight on my face. Not a good thing."

"You should be more careful," he said.

"You think? I paid a lot of money for my new nose. You never said anything. Do you like it?"

He'd known about the surgery. She'd had it when she was twenty. He supposed the smaller nose made her a little prettier, but it wasn't that big a change.

"It's fine," he said.

She laughed. "Be careful. You'll turn my head with all that praise. My nose was huge and now it's just regular."

"You worry too much about being like everybody else. Average is not a goal."

She looked at him. "I haven't had enough coffee for you to be philosophizing. Besides, you don't know anything about normal. You were born rich and you're still rich."

"You're no different."

"True, but we're not talking about me. As a guy, you have different standards to live up or down to. If you have money, then you can be a total loser and you'll still get the girl. But for me it was different. Hence the surgeries."

"You had more than one?" he asked, frowning slightly. He knew only about her nose.

She sat up and leaned toward him. "Breasts," she said in a mock whisper. "I had breast implants."

His gaze involuntarily dropped to her chest. Then he jerked his head to the right and focused on the weight bench next to him.

"Why?" he asked, determined not to think about her body and especially not her breasts, which were suddenly more interesting than he wanted them to be.

"After I lost weight, I discovered I had the chest of a twelve-year-old-boy. I was totally flat. It was depressing. So I got implants. I went for a jumbo B—which seemed about right for my newly skinny self."

She stood and turned sideways in front of the mirror. "I don't know. Sometimes I think I should have just gone for it and ordered the centerfold breasts. What do you think?"

He told himself not to look, but it was like trying to hold back the tide. Against his will, his head turned and his gaze settled on her chest. Meri raised her tank top to show off her sports bra.

"Are they okay, Jack?"

A guy walking by did a double take. "They're great, honey."

She dropped her shirt and smiled. "Thanks."

Jack glanced at the guy and instantly wanted to kill him. It would be fast and relatively painless for the bastard. A quick twist of the neck and he would fall lifeless to the ground.

Meri dropped her shirt. "I love being a girl."

"You're still playing me. I'm going to ignore you."

"I'm not sure you can," she teased. "But you can try. Let's change the subject. We can talk about you. Men love to talk about themselves."

He grabbed a couple of weights and sat on a bench. "Or we could focus on our workout."

"I don't think so." She lay on her back and did chest presses. "What have you been up to for the last ten years? I know you went into the military."

"Army," he said between reps.

"I heard it was Special Forces."

"That, too."

"I also heard you left and started your own company dealing with corporations that want to expand into the dangerous parts of the world."

Apparently he wasn't the only one who had done some research.

"It's impressive," she said. "You've grown that company into quite the business."

"I'm doing okay." Five hundred million in billing in the past year. His accountants kept begging him to go public. They told him he could make a fortune. But he already had more than he needed, and going public meant giving up control.

"Are you married?" she asked.

He looked over at her. She'd shifted positions and was now doing bicep curls. Her honey-tanned skin was slick with sweat, her face flushed, her expression intense. She was totally focused on what she was doing.

Would she be like that in bed? Giving a hundred percent, really going for it?

The thought came from nowhere and he quickly pushed it away. Meri could never be more than Hunter's baby sister. She could dance around naked and beg him to take her—they were never going there.

"Jack? You gonna answer the question?"

Which was? Oh, yeah. "No, I'm not married."

"You're not gay, are you? Hunter always wondered."

He ignored her and the question. If he didn't react, she would get tired of her game and move on to something else.

She sighed. "Okay, that was funny only to me. So there's no wife, but is there someone significant?"

"No."

"Ever been anyone?"

"There have been plenty."

She looked at him. "You know what I mean. A relationship where you're exchanging more than bodily fluids. Have you ever been in love?"

"No," he said flatly. Women tried to get close and he didn't let them.

"Me, either," she said with a sigh. "Which is deeply tragic. I want to be in love. I've been close. I thought I was in love, but now I'm not so sure. I have trust and commitment issues. It's from losing my mom when I was young and then losing Hunter. Isn't it interesting that knowing what the problem is doesn't mean I can fix it?"

He didn't know what to say to that. In his world, people didn't talk about their feelings.

"You lost a brother when you were young," she said. "That had to have affected you."

No way he was thinking about that. He stood. "I'm done. I'm going to take a shower."

She rose and moved close. "Want to take one together?"

He had an instant image of her naked, water pouring over her body. How would she feel? His fingers curled slightly, as if imagining cupping her breasts.

Damn her, he thought. She wasn't going to win. It was time to stop playing nice.

He moved forward, crowding her. She stepped back until she bumped into a weight bench, then she dropped into a sitting position. He crouched in front of her.

"You do not want to play this game with me," he told her in a low voice. "I'm not one of your brainy book guys. I have seen things you can't begin to imagine, I have survived situations you couldn't begin to invent. You may be smart, but this isn't about your brain. You can play me all you want, but eventually there will be consequences. Are you prepared for that, little girl?"

"I'm not a little girl."

He reached behind her and wrapped his hand around her ponytail, pulling just hard enough to force her head back. Then he put his free hand on her throat and stroked the underside of her jaw.

Her eyes widened. He sensed her fighting fear and something else. Something sexual.

He knew because he felt it, too. A pulsing heat that arced between them. Need swirled and grew until he wanted to do a whole lot more than teach her a lesson.

Then she smiled. "I'm getting to you, aren't I?"

He released her. "In your dreams."

* * *

Back at the house, Meri went up to her room to change clothes. She didn't offer to help Jack with his. After their close encounter at the gym, she needed a little time to regroup.

There had been a moment when Jack had touched her that had if not changed everything then certainly captured her attention. A moment when she'd been aware of him as being a powerful man and maybe the slightest bit dangerous.

"I'm not impressed," she told herself as she brushed out her hair, then slipped into a skimpy sundress that left her arms bare. "I'm tough, too." Sort of.

Jack was right. He'd been through things she couldn't begin to imagine. While they'd both changed in the past eleven years, she wondered who had changed more on the inside. Was the man anything like the boy she'd both loved and hated?

Before she could decide, she heard the rumble of a truck engine. A quick glance at her watch told her the delivery was right on time.

"It's here! It's here!" she yelled as she ran out of her room and raced down the stairs. "Jack, you have to come see. It's just totally cool."

She burst out of the house and danced over to the truck. "Were you careful? You were careful, right? It's very expensive and delicate and I can't wait until you set it up. You're going to calibrate it, right? You know how? You've been trained?"

The guy with the clipboard looked at her, then shook his head. "You're a scientist, aren't you?"

"Yes. How'd you know?"

"No one else gets that excited about a telescope." He pointed back at the compact car parked behind the truck. "He calibrates it. I just deliver."

Jack walked outside and joined her. "A telescope?"

"I know—it's too exciting for words. It was very expensive, but the best ones are. You won't believe what we'll be able to see. And it's so clear. How long until sunset?"

She looked at the sky. It would be too long but worth the wait.

"You bought a telescope for the house?" he asked.

"Uh-huh."

"We already have one."

She wrinkled her nose. "It's a toy. This is an instrument."

"But you're only here for a month."

Less if her plan went well. "I know, but I want to see the stars. Everything is better when there are stars to look at."

"You're leaving it in place, aren't you?"

"For the families," she said, watching anxiously as the ramp was lowered on the truck. "I'll write up some instructions, although it's computer-guided. They won't have to do anything but type in what they want to see, then stand back and watch the show. Not that we'll be using the program. I can find whatever you want to see."

"I have no doubt."

She glanced at him. "What?"

"Nothing. Just you."

Which meant what? Not that Jack would tell her if she asked.

"Hunter would have loved this," she said absently, knowing her brother would have made fun of her, then spent the whole night looking at the sky.

Thinking about her brother was both wonderful and filled with pain. While she appreciated all the memories she had, she still had a hole in her heart from his passing.

"I think about him every day," she told Jack. "I think about him and wish he were here. Do you think about him much?"

Jack's expression closed and he turned away. "No. I don't think about him at all."

She knew he couldn't be telling the truth. He and Hunter had been close for a long time. They'd been like brothers. Jack couldn't have forgotten that.

Her instinct to be compassionate battled with her annoyance. Temper won.

"Most people improve with age," she said. "Too bad you didn't. You not only break your word but you're a liar, as well."

Three

Jack spent a couple of hours in the loft office, working. He called his assistant back in Dallas.

"They're building more roads in Afghanistan," Bobbi Sue told him. "They're looking at maybe an eighteen-month contract, but we all know those things take longer. And Sister Helena called. They want to take in another convoy of medical supplies."

His business provided protection in dangerous parts of the world. His teams allowed building crews to get their jobs done and get out. The work was dangerous, often a logistical nightmare and extremely expensive. His corporate clients paid well for what they got.

The corporate profits were channeled into funding protection for those providing relief efforts in places often forgotten. He'd grown up in the shadow of the

Howington Foundation, a philanthropic trust that helped the poor. Jack hated having a number after his name and had vowed he would make his own way.

He had. He'd grown his company from nothing, but he couldn't seem to escape that damn sense of duty. The one that told him he needed to use his profits for something other than a flashy lifestyle.

His critics said he could afford to be generous—he had a trust fund worth nearly a billion dollars. What they didn't know is he never touched it. Another vow he'd made to himself. He'd grown up with something to prove. The question was whether or not he would have achieved enough to let that need go.

"Get Ron on the contract," Jack told his assistant. "The usual clauses. Tell Sister Helena to e-mail the best dates for the convoy and we'll get as close to them as possible."

"She's going to want to leave before you're back from your vacation in Tahoe."

"I'm not on vacation."

"Hmm, a month in a fancy house with nothing to do with your time? Sounds like a vacation to me."

"I'm working."

"Talk, talk, talk."

Bobbi Sue had attitude, which he put up with because she was the best at her job. She was also old enough to be his mother, a fact she mentioned on a regular basis, especially when she hounded him on the topic of settling down.

"Someone else will have to take Sister Helena's team in," he said. "See if Wade's available." Wade was one of his best guys.

"Will do. Anything else?"

"Not from my end."

"You know, I looked up Hunter's Landing on the Internet, and the place you're staying isn't that far from the casinos."

"I'm aware of that."

"So you should go. Gamble, talk to some people. You spend too much time alone."

He thought about Meri, sleeping in the room next to his. "Not anymore."

"Does that mean you're seeing someone?"

"No."

"You need to get married."

"You need to get off me."

Bobbi Sue sighed. "All right, but just in the short term."

Jack hung up. He glanced at his computer, but for once he didn't want to work. He paced the length of the spacious bedroom, ignoring the fireplace, the view and the television. Then he went downstairs to confront the woman who seemed determined to think the worst of him.

Not that he cared what she thought. But this wasn't about her—it was about Hunter.

He found Meri in the kitchen, sitting on the counter, eating ice cream out of a pint-size container.

"Lunch?" he asked as he entered the room.

"Sort of. Not exactly high in nutrition, but I'm more interested in sugar and fat right now."

He stared at her miniature spoon. "That's an interesting size."

She waved the tiny utensil. "It's my ice-cream-eating spoon. I try to avoid using food as an emotional crutch, but sometimes ice cream is the only solution. I use this spoon because it takes longer to eat and I have a better chance of getting disgusted with myself and stopping before finishing the pint. A trick for keeping off the weight. I have a thousand of them."

"This situation required ice cream?"

She licked the spoon. He did his best to ignore the flick of her tongue and the sigh that followed, along with the rush of unwelcome heat in his body.

"You pissed me off," she told him.

Translation: he'd hurt her. Hunter was her brother. She wouldn't want to think his friends had forgotten him.

He leaned against the counter as he considered what to do. His natural inclination was to walk away. Her feelings didn't matter to him. At least they shouldn't. But this was Meri, and he was supposed to be looking out for her. Which meant not making a bad situation worse.

Maybe a small concession was in order. "I don't want to think about Hunter," he admitted. "I've trained myself not to. But he's there. All the time."

She eyed him. "Why should I believe you?"

"I don't care if you do."

She surprised him by smiling. "Okay. I like that answer. If you'd tried to convince me, I would have known you were just placating me. But your stick-up-the-butt attitude is honest."

"Excuse me?"

"You're excused."

He frowned. Had she always been this irritating?

"You getting much work done?" she asked as she checked her watch. "I'm not. There's so much going on right now and I really need to focus. But it's tough. Being here, seducing you—it's a full time job."

He folded his arms over his chest. "You need to let that go."

"The seduction part? I don't think so. I'm making progress. You're going on the defensive. What happened in the gym was definitely about taking charge. So that means I'm getting to you." She held out the ice cream container. "Want some, big guy?"

She was mocking him. She was irreverent and fearless and determined. All good qualities, but not in this situation. She was right. He wanted to get control. And he could think of only one way to do that.

He moved close and took the ice cream from her. After setting it and the spoon on the counter, he cupped her face and kissed her.

He took rather than asked. He claimed her with his lips, branding her skin with his own. He leaned in, crowding her, showing her that she hadn't thought her plan through.

She stiffened slightly and gasped in surprise. He took advantage of the moment and plunged his tongue into her mouth.

She was cool from the ice cream, cool with a hint of fire. She tasted of chocolate and something that had to be her own erotic essence. He ignored the softness of her skin, the sensual feel of her mouth and the heat that poured through him.

She pulled back slightly and gazed into his eyes. "Is that the best you can do?" she asked before she put her arms around his neck and drew him in.

She kissed him back with a need that surprised him. She opened for him and then met his tongue with darting licks of her own.

She'd parted her legs, so he slipped between her thighs. Although she was much shorter, with her sitting on the counter, he found himself nestled against her crotch.

Blood pumped, making him hard. Desire consumed him. Desire for a woman he couldn't have. Dammit all to hell.

Then he reminded himself that his reaction was to an attractive woman. It wasn't specific. It wasn't about Meri. As his assistant enjoyed pointing out, he'd been solitary for a long time. Even brief sexual encounters no longer intrigued him. He'd been lost in a world of work and nothing else.

He had needs. That was all this was—a scratch for an itch.

He pulled back. "Interesting."

She raised her eyebrows. "It was a whole lot more than interesting and you know it."

"If it's important for you to believe that, go ahead."

"I don't mind that you're not making this easy," she told him. "The victory will be all the sweeter." She picked up her ice cream and put the cover back. "I'm done."

"Sugar and fat needs met?"

"I no longer need the comfort. My bad mood is gone."

So like a woman, he thought as he leaned against the counter. "Because I kissed you?"

She smiled and jumped to the floor, then walked to the freezer. "Because you liked it."

He wasn't going to argue the point.

She closed the freezer door with her hip, then looked at him. "Tell me about the women in your life."

"Not much to tell."

"It's tough, isn't it?" She leaned against the counter opposite his. For once, her eyes weren't bright with humor or challenge. "Being who we are and trying to get involved. The money thing, I mean."

Because they both came from money. Because they'd been raised with the idea that they had to be careful, to make sure they didn't fall for someone who was in it for the wrong reasons.

Without wanting to, Jack remembered sitting in on a painful conversation between Hunter and Meredith. He'd tried to escape more than once, but his friend had wanted him to stick around to make sure Meri really listened.

"Guys are going to know who you are," Hunter had told her. "You have to be smart and not just think with your heart."

Meri had been sixteen. She'd writhed in her seat as Hunter had talked, then she'd stood and glared at him. "Who is going to want me for anything else?" she demanded. "I'm not pretty. I'll never be pretty. I'm nothing more than a giant brain with braces and a big nose. I'm going to have to buy all my boyfriends."

Hunter had looked at Jack with an expression that begged for help, but Jack hadn't known what to say either. They were too young to be guiding Meri through life—what experiences did they have to pass on? Doing twins from the law school hardly counted.

"I have it easier than you do," he said, forcing himself back to the present, not wanting to think about how he'd failed both Hunter and Meri. "The women I go out with don't know who I am."

"Interesting point. I don't talk about my family, but word gets out. I've actually reached the point in my life where I have to have men investigated before I start dating them. It's not fun."

"You're doing the right thing." Not that she was the only one checking out her dates. He ran a check on all of them, too. For casual dates, he only bothered with a preliminary investigation, but if it looked like things were getting serious, he asked for a more involved report.

She glanced at her watch again.

"You have an appointment?" he asked.

She grinned. "I have a surprise."

"Another one?"

"Oh, yeah. So there's no little woman waiting in the wings?"

"I told you—I'm not the little-woman type."

"Of course. You're the kind of man who enjoys a challenge. Which is what I am."

Okay, so kissing her hadn't gotten her to back off. He needed another direction. He refused to spend the next three and a half weeks dodging Meri. All he needed was a plan. He'd never been defeated before and he wasn't about to be defeated now.

"But I want something different from the men in my life," she continued. "Maybe my tastes have matured, but I'm looking for someone smart and funny—but normal-smart. Not brainy. I could never marry another genius. We'd have a mutant child, for sure."

He chuckled. "Your own version of genetic engineering?"

"Sort of. I made a list of characteristics that are important to me. I used to have a whole program I wrote one weekend, but that seemed so calculated. A list is more ordinary."

"Not if you wrote it in binary code."

She rolled her eyes. "Oh, please. I'd never do that. C++ maybe."

He was going to guess C++ was another computer language, but he could be wrong.

"Not that I needed a computer program to know Andrew is a great guy."

Jack stared at her. "Andrew?"

"The man I've been dating for a while now. He checked out great, and things are getting serious."

Jack didn't remember hearing about any guy named Andrew. Not that he got personally involved unless things were heating up—which, apparently, they were. Why hadn't he been told?

"How serious?" he asked as he heard the sound of a truck heading toward the house.

"I'm probably going to marry him," Meri said, then ran out of the kitchen. "You hear that? They're here!"

Marry him?

Before he could react to that, he found himself following her to the foyer and beyond that to the front of the house. A shuttle van pulled to a stop in front of the porch, and the door eased open.

"Who's here?" he asked, but Meri wasn't listening. She bounced from foot to foot, then threw herself into the arms of the first person off the shuttle. He was short, skinny and wearing glasses thick enough to be portholes. Nothing about him was the least bit threatening, and Jack immediately wanted to kill him.

"You made it," Meri said, hugging the guy again. "I've missed you so much."

The guy disentangled himself. "It's been a week, Meri. You need to get out more."

She laughed, then turned to the next person and greeted him with exactly the same enthusiasm. Okay. So nerd guy wasn't Andrew. Good to know.

Meri welcomed all eight visitors with exactly the same amount of enthusiasm, then she turned to Jack.

"Everybody, this is Jack. Jack, this is my team."

"Team for what?" he asked.

She grinned. "Would you believe me if I said polo?"

Judging from their pale skin and slightly peering gazes, he was going to guess none of them had ever seen a horse outside of the movies or television.

"No."

"I didn't think so. This is my solid-rocket-fuel team. We're working on ways to make it less toxic and more efficient. There's a technical explanation, but I don't want to watch your eyes glaze over."

"I appreciate that. What are they doing here?"

"Don't freak. They're not all staying in the house. Only Colin and Betina. The rest are staying at nearby hotels."

Jack didn't like the idea of anyone else hanging around. He needed to concentrate on work. Of course, if Meri were distracted by her friends, she wouldn't be such a problem for him.

"Why are they here?" he asked.

"So we can work. I can't leave the mountain, so they agreed to a field trip." She leaned toward him and lowered her voice. "I know you're going to find it difficult to believe, but this is a really fun group."

Most of her colleagues were squinting in the sun and looking uncomfortable. "I can only imagine."

She walked over to the oldest woman in the group—a slightly overweight, stylishly dressed blonde—linked arms with her and led her forward.

"Jack, this is my friend Betina. Technically she's a liaison—she stands between the team and the real world, taking care of all the details the scientifically gifted seem to be so bad with. In reality, she's my best friend and the reason I'm just so darned normal."

He eyed the other woman and wondered how many of Meri's secrets she knew.

"Nice to meet you," he said as he shook hands with Betina.

Betina smiled. "I'm enjoying meeting you, as well," she said. "Finally."

Finally?

Meri grinned. "Did I tell you or what?"

Tell her what? But before Jack could ask, the group went into the house. He was left standing on the porch, wondering when the hell his life had gotten so out of his control.

Meri sat cross-legged in the center of the bed while her friend unpacked. "He's gorgeous. Admit it—you saw it."

Betina smiled. "Jack is very nice-looking, if you

enjoy the tall, dark and powerful type. He wasn't happy about us arriving."

"I know. I didn't tell him you were coming. It was fabulous. I wish you'd seen the look on his face when I explained why you were here. Of course, it was right after I told him I might marry Andrew, so there it was a double-thrill moment for me."

Betina unpacked her cosmetics and carried them into the attached bathroom. "You know you're not marrying Andrew. You're baiting Jack."

"It's fun and I need a hobby." Meri flopped back on the bed. "Why shouldn't I bait him? He deserves it. He was mean to me."

"He was in college. At that age, men are not known for their emotional sensitivity. Actually, they're not known for it at any age. But the point is, you bared your heart and soul and he reacted badly. I agree some punishment is in order, but you're taking it all too far. This is a mistake, Meri."

Meri loved Betina like a sister...sometimes like a mom. There were only twelve years between them chronologically, but in life experiences they were light-years apart.

Betina had been the project manager's assistant at the think tank that had first hired Meri. The second week Meri had been there, Betina had walked into her lab.

"Do you have anything close to a sense of humor?" the other woman had asked. "I don't mind that you're brilliant, but a sense of humor is required for any kind of a relationship."

Meri hadn't known what to say. She'd been eighteen

and terrified of living on her own in a strange city. Money wasn't an issue—the think tank had hired her for more than she'd ever thought she would earn and she had a family trust fund. But she'd spent that last third of her life in college. What did she know about furnishing an apartment, buying a car, paying bills?

"I don't know if I would qualify as funny," Meri had said honestly. "Does sarcasm count?"

Betina had smiled. "Oh, honey, sarcasm is the best."

At that moment their friendship had been born.

Betina had been turning thirty and on her own for over a decade. She'd shown Meri how to live on her own and had insisted she buy a condo in a good part of D.C.

She'd taken care of Meri after both her surgeries, offered fashion advice, love life advice and had hooked her up with a trainer who had pummeled her into shape.

"Why is getting revenge a mistake?" Meri asked as her friend finished unpacking. "He's earned it."

"Because you're not thinking this through. You're going to get into trouble and I don't want that to happen. Your relationship with Jack isn't what you think."

Meri frowned. "What do you mean? I totally understand my feelings about Jack. I had a huge crush on him, he hurt me and, because of that, I've been unable to move on. If I sleep with him, I'll instantly figure out that he's not special at all. He's just some guy and I'll be healed. The benefit is I get to leave him wanting more."

Betina sat next to her and fluffed her short hair. "I hate travel. I always get puffy." Then she drew in a breath. "You didn't have a crush on Jack. You were in love with him then and you're still in love with him.

You're emotionally connected to him, even if you refuse to admit it. Sleeping with him is only going to confuse the matter. The problem with your plan is that, odds are, the person left wanting more could easily be you."

Meri sat up and took Betina's hands. "I love and admire you, but you are desperately wrong."

"I hope so, for your sake."

But her friend sounded worried as she spoke. Meri appreciated the show of support. They were never going to agree on this topic. Better to move on.

She released Betina's hands and grinned. "So Colin is right next door. Whatever will the two of you get up to late at night?"

Betina flushed. "Lower your voice," she whispered. "He'll hear you."

"Oh, please. He wouldn't hear a nuclear explosion if he was focused on something else, and when I walked by his room, he was already booting his laptop. We're safe. Don't you love how I got the two of you into the house while everyone else is far, far away?"

"I guess," Betina said with uncharacteristic indecision. "I know something has to happen soon or I'll be forced to back the car over him. He's such a sweetie. And you know I really like him, but I don't think I'm his type."

Meri groaned. "He doesn't have a type. He's a nerd. Do you think he dates much?"

"He should. He's adorable and smart and funny."

Her friend had it bad, Meri thought happily. And she was pretty sure that Colin found Betina equally intriguing. Usually Betina simply took what she wanted in the man department. But something about Colin made her nervous.

"He's afraid of being rejected," Meri told her. "Something I can relate to."

"I wouldn't reject him," Betina said. "But it will never work. We're on a project together. I'm too old for him and I'm too fat."

"You're six years older, which is nothing, and you're not fat. You're totally curvy and lush. Guys go for that."

They always had. Meri had spent the last decade marveling at the number of men her friend met, dated, slept with and dumped.

"Not Colin. He barely speaks to me."

"Which is interesting," Meri said. "He talks to everyone else."

It was true. Colin was tongue-tied around Betina. Meri thought it was charming.

At first, when her friend had confessed her interest in Colin, Meri had been protective of her coworker. Colin might enjoy the ride that was Betina, but once dumped, he would be heartbroken. Then Betina had admitted her feelings went a whole lot deeper. The L word had been whispered.

After getting over the idea of her friend being in love with anyone, Meri had agreed to help. So far, she'd been unable to think of a way to bring the couple together. Hunter's lodge had offered the perfect opportunity.

"You have time," Meri pointed out. "Jack and I never come down here, so you have the whole floor to yourselves. You can talk to each other in a casual setting. No pressure. It will be great."

Betina smiled. "Hey, it's *my* job to be the positive, self-actualized one."

"I know. I love being the emotionally mature friend. It doesn't happen often."

"It happens more and more."

Meri leaned in and hugged her friend. "You're the best."

"So are you."

Jack looked up as he heard footsteps on the stairs. Seconds later, Meri appeared in his loft office.

She'd changed into a tight skirt and cropped top, curled her hair and put on makeup. Always pretty, she'd upped the stakes to come-get-me sexy.

A quick bit of research on the Internet had told him that the guy she'd mentioned wasn't one of her scientists. Instead he worked for a D.C. lobbyist and was safely several thousand miles away. Not that Jack cared one way or the other. The only issue for him was researching the man more thoroughly. If things were getting serious, it was his job to make sure Meri wasn't being taken.

His low-grade anger was something he would deal with later. He didn't know why he minded the thought of her marrying some guy, but he did.

"We're going to dinner," she announced when she stopped in front of his desk. "You might not believe this, but we're actually a pretty fun group. You're welcome to join us."

"Thanks, but no."

"Want me to bring back something? The fridge is still fully stocked, but I could stop for chicken wings."

"I'm good."

She turned to leave. He stopped her with, "You should have mentioned you were engaged."

She turned back to him. "Why? You claim you're not sleeping with me. What would an engagement matter one way or another?"

"It makes a difference. I wouldn't have kissed you."

"Ah. Then I'm glad you didn't know." Her blue eyes brightened with amusement. "Does the fact that I belong to someone else make me more tempting? The allure of the forbidden?"

He had to consciously keep from smiling. She'd always been overly dramatic.

"No," he told her. "Sorry."

"You're not sorry. And, for what it's worth, the engagement isn't official. I wouldn't be trying to sleep with you if I'd said yes."

A cool rush of relief swept through him. "You said no?"

"I didn't say anything. Andrew hasn't actually proposed. I found a ring." She shifted on her high heels. "I didn't know what to think. I'd never thought about getting married. I realized we had unfinished business, so here I am. Seducing you."

He ignored that. "You're sleeping with him." The point was obvious, so he didn't make it a question.

She leaned forward and sighed. "It bothers you, doesn't it? Thinking about me in bed with another man. Writhing, panting, being taken." She straightened and fanned herself. "Wow, it's really warm here at the top of the house."

He didn't react, at least not on the outside. But her words had done what she'd wanted them to do. He reacted on the inside, with heat building in his groin.

She got to him. He would give her points for that. But she wouldn't win.

"So no on dinner?" she asked.

"I have work."

"Okay. Want a goodbye kiss before I go?"

He hated that he did. He wanted to feel her mouth on his, her body leaning in close. He wanted skin on skin, touching her until he made her cry out with a passion she couldn't control. "No, thanks," he said coolly.

She eyed him for a second, then grinned. "We both know that's not true, don't we, Jack?"

And then she was gone.

Four

Meri arrived home from dinner with her team feeling just full enough, with a slight buzz. They'd taken the shuttle van into town, and that had meant no one had to be a designated driver. Wine had flowed freely. Well, as freely as it could given no one drank more than a glass, preferring the thrill of intellectual discussion to the mental blurriness of too much alcohol.

But just this once Meri had passed up the wine and gone with a margarita. That was fine, but she'd ordered a second one and was absolutely feeling it as she climbed the stairs to her bedroom.

As she reached the landing, she saw two doors and was reminded that it was also the same floor with Jack's bedroom.

What an interesting fact, she thought as she paused

and stared at the firmly closed door. He was in there. By himself, she would guess. So what exactly was he getting up to?

She was pretty confident he was stretched out on the bed, watching TV or reading. But this was her buzz, and she could imagine him waiting for her in the massive tub in front of the fireplace if she wanted to. Because in her fantasy, he wanted her with a desperation that took his breath away. In her fantasy, he was deeply sorry for hurting her and he'd spent the past eleven years barely surviving because his love for her had been so great it had immobilized him.

"Okay, that last one is total crap," she whispered to herself. "But the other two have possibilities."

She walked to his door, knocked once, then let herself in before he could tell her to go away.

A quick glance around the room told her that he wasn't about to fulfill her bathtub fantasy. Probably for the best. She was really feeling the margarita, and drowning was a distinct possibility.

Instead of being naked and in water, Jack sat in a corner chair, his feet up on the leather ottoman, reading. At least he'd been reading until she'd walked in. Now he set the book on his lap and looked at her expectantly.

She swayed as she moved toward the bed and sank down on the edge. She pushed off her sandals and smiled at him.

"Dinner was great. You should have come."

"I'll survive the deep loss."

She smiled. "You're so funny. Sometimes I forget you're funny. I think it's because you're so intense and macho. Dangerous. You were always dangerous. Before, it was just about who you were as a person, but now you have access to all kinds of weapons. Doubly dangerous."

His gaze narrowed slightly. "You're drunk."

She waved her left hand back and forth. "*Drunk* is such a strong term. Tipsy. Buzzed. Seriously buzzed. I had a second margarita. Always a mistake. I don't drink much, so I never build up any tolerance. And I'm small, so there's not much in the way of body mass. I could figure out the formula if you want. How many ounces of alcohol per pound of human body."

"An intriguing offer, but no."

She smiled. "It's the math, huh. You're scared of the math. Most people are. I don't know why. Math is constant, you know. It's built on principles, and once you learn them, they don't change. It's not like literature. That's open to interpretation and there's all that writing. But math is clean. You're right or you're not. I like being right."

"It's your competitive streak," he said.

She swayed slightly on the bed. "You think I'm competitive?"

"It's in your blood."

"I guess. I like to be right about stuff. I get focused. I can be a real pain." She grinned. "Doesn't that make me even cuter? How can you stand it?"

"I'm using every ounce of willpower not to attack you this very moment."

"You're so lying, but it's sweet. Thank you."

She stared at him. If eyes were the windows to the

soul, then Jack's innermost place was a dark and protected place.

Secrets, she thought. They all had secrets. What were his?

Not that he would tell her. He kept that sort of thing to himself. But if he ever did decide to trust someone, it would be forever, she thought idly. Or maybe that was another of her fantasies.

"You need to help me with Betina and Colin," she told him. "We're going to get them together."

One dark eyebrow rose. "I don't think so."

"Oh, come on. Don't be such a guy. This could be fun. Just think of it—we could be part of a great love match."

"Colin and Betina?" He sounded doubtful.

"Sure. Betina has a serious thing for Colin. I was skeptical at first because Betina changes her men with the rhythm of the tide. A long-term relationship for her is a week. But that's because she's afraid to really care about someone. She had a bad early marriage years ago. Anyway, she's liked Colin for a long time, and that liking has grown into something more. Something significant."

She paused, waiting for him to grasp the importance of the information. Obviously he missed it, because he said, "I'm not getting involved."

"You have to. It's not like you're doing anything else with your time."

"We're going to ignore my work and the effort I put into avoiding you?"

"Oh, yeah. There's hard duty. A beautiful single woman desperately wants you in her bed. Poor Jack. Your life is pain."

She could think of a thousand ways he could have reacted, but she never expected him to smile.

"You think of yourself as beautiful?" he asked quietly, sounding almost pleased.

Meri shifted on the bed. "It was a figure of speech."

"The last time we talked about your appearance, you said you were a freak."

She didn't want to think about that, but if he insisted... "The last time we talked about my appearance, you emotionally slapped me, trampled my heart and left me for dead."

His smile faded. "I'm sorry. I should have handled that differently."

"But you didn't. I wasn't asking for sex right that moment." She didn't want to be talking about this. It was too humiliating. "My point is, Betina is crazy about Colin and I'm pretty sure he likes her. Which is where you come in. I want you to find out for sure."

"What? No."

"Why not? You're a guy, he's a guy. You can ask him if he likes Betina."

"Should I pass you a note in homeroom?"

"I don't care how I get the information, I just need confirmation."

"You're not getting it from me."

She remembered his being stubborn but never this bad. "Have I mentioned you're annoying? Because you are."

"I live to serve."

"If only that were true. Look, they're both great people. They deserve to be happy. I'm just giving them a little push."

"Did you need a push with Andrew?"

She sighed. "I wondered when you'd bring him up."

"You're nearly engaged. Why wouldn't I be curious?"

She tried to figure out what he was thinking from his tone of voice, but as usual, Jack gave nothing away. It was one of his more annoying characteristics.

"We met at a charity auction," she said. "There was a pet fashion show to start things off. Somehow I got tangled up in the leashes and nearly fell. Andrew rescued me. It was very romantic."

"I can only imagine."

She ignored any hint of sarcasm in his voice. Maybe knowing there was another man in her life would make him a little less arrogant.

"He was funny and charming and I liked him right away. We have so much in common. What movies we like, where we go on vacation. It's been really fun."

It *had* been fun, she thought, remembering all the good times with Andrew. But she'd been on this coast for nearly six months. They'd had a chance to get together only a few times, although they talked regularly. Their relationship seemed to be on hold and she obviously didn't mind. Something she was going to have to think about.

"Is he a genius, too?" Jack asked.

"No, he's delightfully normal. Smart but not too smart. I like that in a guy."

"What do you know about him? Did you check him out?"

"Of course. He's just a regular guy. Not in it for money." Her good mood faded. "Is that your point? That no one could possibly want me if it wasn't for the money?"

"Not at all. I just want you to be happy."

"I am happy. Blissfully so. Andrew's the one. We'll be engaged as soon as I get back to D.C." Which wasn't actually true but it sounded good.

"Congratulations."

Jack had ruined everything, she thought bitterly as she stood. Her buzz, her great evening.

"Just because you don't believe in letting yourself care about people doesn't mean the feelings aren't real," she told him. "Some of us want to connect."

"I hope you do. I hope this is everything you want."

"Why don't I believe you? What aren't you saying?"

"That if Andrew was so important to you, you wouldn't stay away from him for six months."

She walked to the door. "Who says I have?"

With that, she walked out and closed the door behind her.

It was only a few steps to her room, and she was grateful for the solitary quiet when she entered. After flicking on a few lights, she crossed to the window and stared out at the night sky.

It was a perfect night for viewing the stars, but she wasn't in the mood. Not even on her brand-new telescope. She hurt too much and it was hard to say why.

Maybe because Jack was right. If Andrew was that important to her, she wouldn't stay away from him for six months. But she had, and it had been relatively easy. Too easy. If she were really in love with him, wouldn't she be desperate to be with him?

Finding the engagement ring had shocked her. She hadn't known what to think about his proposing. She'd been happy, but a part of her had known that it was time to put off the inevitable. That closure with Jack was required.

She'd known about Hunter's friends coming to stay at the house. She'd taken the consulting job in California, hired on as the caretaker of the house and had waited to confront the man who was holding her back. Once she got her revenge on Jack, she would be fine.

"That's what's wrong," she whispered to herself. "I'm still waiting to punish him. Once Jack is reduced to dust, I'll be able to give my whole heart to Andrew. It's just going to be another week or so. Then I'll be happy."

Jack spent a restless night. He told himself it was because he'd had coffee too late in the day, but part of the problem was Meri's words. Her claim that he didn't connect.

Late the next morning, he saved the files on his computer and opened the top desk drawer in his temporary office. There was an envelope inside, along with a letter.

The letter had been waiting for him the first day he'd arrived. He'd recognized the distinctive handwriting and had known it was from Matt. The battered appliances in the kitchen had been another clue. His friend might be able to program a computer to do heart surgery, but Matt couldn't do something simple like work an electric can opener.

For some reason, Jack had avoided the letter. Now he opened the envelope and pulled out the single sheet of paper.

Jack—

When I read Ryan's note that called this place a "love shack," my first thought was, what a load of BS. But now I think he may have been onto something. He was also right about how wrong we were when we compiled our universal truths about women. Remember those? Yeah? Well, now you can forget 'em. We had no idea.

As for me, here's what I learned during my month at the cabin: the most important work you'll ever do has nothing to do with the job. And it's work you can't do by yourself. But when you find a partner you can trust and the two of you do that work together, it pays better than any career you could imagine. And the perks? You have no idea....

Have a good month, pal.

Matt.

Jack read the letter again. He'd figured out a long time ago that he didn't know squat about women. Not that it mattered, as he never got involved. As for Matt and his other friends, sometimes he allowed himself to miss them. To wonder what it would have been like if Hunter hadn't died. Because Hunter was the one who had held them all together. Without him, they'd gone their separate ways. There were times when he—

He stood and shook his head. Okay, he needed more coffee or something, because there was no way he was spending the rest of the morning in his head.

He went downstairs and poured himself coffee. He could hear Meri and her team talking in the dining room.

"String theory is ruining theoretical physics," one of the guys said. "Everything has to be defined and explained, which is wasting a lot of time. Sure there's a why and a how, but if there's no practical application, then why bother?"

"Because you can't know the practical application until you understand the theory."

"It's not a theory. It's equations. Compare string theory to something else. Something like—"

They kept on talking, but even thought Jack knew they were probably speaking English, he had no idea what they were saying. He knew string theory had nothing to do with strings and maybe something to do with the universe. The word *vibrating* was attached to the idea in his head, but whether that meant string theory was about vibrations in the universe or just so above him that it made his teeth hurt, he wasn't sure.

"All very interesting," Meri said loudly over the argument. "But it has little to do with the project at hand. Get back to work. All of you."

There was a little grumbling, but the discussion shifted back to something that sounded a lot like solid rocket fuel. Not that Jack could be sure.

After grabbing his mug, he stepped out onto the deck. Hunter would be proud of Meri. She'd turned into a hell of a woman.

He pulled out his cell phone and hit redial. Bobbi Sue answered on the first ring. "You've got to stop calling me," she told him by way of greeting. "I swear, you're starting to get on my nerves. We're all capable here. We can do the job. You're just bored, and let me tell you, I don't like being punished for your mood swings."

He ignored her. "I want you to check out someone Meri's seeing. Andrew Layman. His address is on file. I want to know everything about him. Apparently it's gotten serious, and I want to make sure Meri isn't getting involved with a guy after her money."

"I swear, Jack, you have got to stop spying on this girl. If you're so interested, date her yourself. Otherwise get out of her life."

"I can't. She's a wealthy heiress. That makes her a target. Besides, I gave my word."

"I wish you were here so you could see how unimpressed I am by you giving your word. This just isn't healthy." Bobbi Sue sighed. "I'll do it, but only because it's my job and, for the most part, I respect you."

He grinned, knowing Meri would adore his secretary. "Your praise is all that matters."

"As if I'd believe that. This'll take a couple of days."

"I'm not going anywhere."

"I hear that. You need to get out. Find a woman. I mean it, Jack. Either get involved with Meri or leave the poor girl alone. You have no right to do this."

"I have every right." Meri might not know it, but she needed him. Someone had to keep her safe.

He hung up and returned to the kitchen for more coffee. Meri entered from the dining room.

"Hi. How's your day going?" she asked as she pushed past him and walked into the pantry. "Have you seen the box of pencils I put in here? Colin insists on fresh pencils when he works. Betina thinks it's charming, but I have to tell you, his little quirks are a pain in the butt. There was a whole new box. I swear."

He heard her rummaging around, then she gasped. He stepped to the pantry door and saw her crouched by the bottom shelf.

"What?" he demanded. "Did you hit your head?"

"No," she whispered and slowly straightened. She held a box in her hand, but it wasn't pencils. Instead it was a shoe box covered with childish stickers of unicorns and stars and rainbows.

"This is mine," she breathed. "I haven't seen it in years. I'd forgotten about it. How did it get here?"

As he didn't know what "it" was, he only shrugged.

Meri looked up at him, her eyes filled with tears. "It's pictures of Hunter and my mom and all of us."

She set the box on the counter and opened the top. There were old Polaroid photos of a very young Hunter standing in front of some church. Probably in Europe. He looked about fourteen or fifteen. He had his arm around a much younger Meredith.

"God, I miss him," Meri whispered. "He was my family."

Betina walked into the kitchen. "It's pencils, Meri. You're supposed to be the smart one. Are you telling me you can't find a—" Betina stopped. "What happened?" She turned on Jack. "What the hell did you do to her?"

"Nothing," Meri said before he could defend himself. "It's not him. Look."

Betina moved close and took the photo. "That's you. Is that Hunter?"

"Uh-huh. I think we're in France." She pulled out more pictures. "I can't believe it. Look at how fat I am. Did anyone stop to say, 'Gee, honey, you should eat less'?"

"Food is love," Betina told her and fanned out the pictures on the counter. "You're adorable and Hunter is quite the hunk."

Several more members of Meri's team wandered into the kitchen. Soon they, too, were looking over pictures and talking about Hunter as if they'd known him.

Jack hung back. As much as he wanted to see his friend, he didn't want to open old wounds. For a second he wondered if Meri would need comforting, then he looked at all the people around her. She didn't need him at all. Which was for the best. He didn't want to get involved.

Meri paid the driver, then carried the bag of Chinese food into the house. "Dinner," she yelled in the general direction of the stairs, not sure if Jack would come down or not. She was gratified to see him walk into the kitchen a couple of minutes later.

"Why aren't you out with the nerd brigade?" he asked as she pulled a couple of plates out of the cupboard.

"Nerd brigade?" She smiled. "They'd like that. It sounds very military. They're all going to a club in Lake Tahoe and I'm not in the mood. Plus, I knew you were lonely, so I stayed home to keep you company."

"I'm not lonely."

He sounded annoyed as he spoke, which made her want to giggle. Jack was really easy to rile. It was that stick up his butt—if he would just let it go, he could be a regular person. Of course, his macho I'm-in-charge attitude was part of his appeal.

"Can you reach those?" she asked, pointing to the tall glasses some idiot had put on the top shelf. She could never have left them there.

While he got them for her, she carried the plates and food over to the table in the kitchen, then went to the refrigerator for a couple of beers.

When they were seated across from each other, she said, "So are we invading you too badly?"

"Do you care if you are?"

She considered the question and went with the honest answer. "Not really, but it seemed polite to ask."

"Good to know. I'm getting work done."

"Your company specializes in protecting corporations in scary parts of the world, right?"

He nodded.

"An interesting choice," she said. "But then, you have all that Special Forces training."

Again with the look.

She passed him the kung pao chicken. "I know a few things," she said.

"Yes, that's what my company does. When I left the Army, I wanted to start my own firm. Being a consultant didn't give me enough control. Someone has to rebuild roads in places like Iraq, and our job is to keep those people safe."

"Sounds dangerous."

"We know what we're doing."

"Weren't you supposed to be a lawyer?" she asked.

"I joined the Army after Hunter died."

An interesting way to cope with grief, she thought. But then, maybe the point had been to be so busy he could just forget.

"What do your parents have to say about all this?"

"They're still hoping I'll take over the Howington Foundation."

"Will you?" she asked.

"Probably not. I'm not the foundation type."

She wasn't either, but so far it wasn't an option. Her father seemed content to spend his money on the very young women in his life. Hunter's foundation ran smoothly. She had her trust fund, which she never touched, and a nice salary that covered all of her needs. If Hunter were still alive…

"You have to deal with your grief sometime," she said.

"About the foundation? I'm over it."

"No. Hunter."

Jack's mouth twisted. "I've dealt. Thanks for asking."

"I don't think so. There's a whole lot there under the surface." He'd let down his best friend. That had to bug him. Jack had let her down, too, but for once she wasn't mad at him. Maybe because she'd had a good cry after looking at all the pictures she'd found and felt emotionally cleansed.

She looked at him. "On my bad days I tell myself you're a selfish bastard who played us all. On my good days I tell myself you wanted to stay but couldn't handle what you were going through. Which is it?"

"Both."

* * *

Meri waited until nearly midnight, then climbed the stairs to Jack's office, prepared to let herself out onto the balcony and enjoy the beauty of the heavens. She didn't expect to find him on his laptop.

"You're not supposed to be here," she grumbled as he glanced up. "It's late. You need your rest."

"I see you've changed your seduction techniques. These are interesting. Less effective, in case you were wondering."

"I'm not here to seduce you. I have more important things to do with my time."

He glanced out the French doors toward the sky. "I see. And I would get in the way?"

"You're going to ask a lot of irritating questions. You won't be able to help it. I'll try to be patient, but I'll snap and then you'll get your feelings hurt. I'm just not in the mood to deal with your emotional outbursts."

Instead she wanted to stare at the sky and let the vast beauty heal her soul. Okay, yes, getting Jack into bed was her ultimate goal, but there was a time and place for work and this wasn't it.

"I suspect my feelings will survive just fine," he said.

"No way. You'll go all girlie on me."

She shouldn't have said it. She knew that. She hadn't actually meant to challenge him—she was simply impatient to get out into the night and use the telescope.

He stood without speaking and moved around the desk until he was standing in front of her. Looming, actually. She had to tilt her head all the way back to see into his eyes.

"You think I'm girlie?" he asked in a low, slightly dangerous voice. A voice thick with power. A voice that made her realize he was a whole lot bigger than her and that there were a couple of floors between her and help.

"Not at all," she said quickly. "I didn't mean to say it. The words just slipped out. Bad me. You should probably stalk out and teach me what for by leaving me alone."

Instead he tucked a strand of hair behind her ear. "Do you play all the men in your life?"

She swallowed. "Pretty much."

"Does it work?"

"Mostly."

"Not this time."

He cupped her cheek with his hand, bent down and kissed her.

She'd sensed he was going to and should have had time to brace herself. It was just a kiss, right? No big deal. They'd kissed before, and while she'd liked it, she'd managed to keep perfect control…sort of.

But not this time. The second his mouth touched hers, she started dissolving from the inside out. Technically that couldn't be true, but it *felt* true. Heat poured through her, making her want to move closer. Again something that didn't make sense. The closer she got to Jack, the more their shared body temperature would rise. Wait—it wouldn't rise exactly, it would…

He moved his mouth against hers. This wasn't the angry, something-to-prove kiss he'd given her at the gym. That had been easy to deal with. This kiss was different. It offered instead of taking. He applied just enough pressure to make her want to lean in and do a little demanding of her own.

Without meaning to, she reached up and rested her hands on his shoulders. He pulled her close until they were touching all over. Shoulder to knee, man to woman. He was hard and unyielding, a combination she found wildly erotic.

One of his hands slipped through her hair, tangling in the waves. The other moved up and down her back. Slowly, so slowly. Not touching anything significant, but still...touching.

He continued to brush his mouth against hers, keeping the kiss chaste yet arousing her until she wanted to grab him, shake him and tell him to get on with it already.

When he licked her bottom lip, she nearly groaned in relief. Fortunately she managed to hold in the sound. She even waited a nanosecond before parting for him. She didn't want to seem *too* eager. But then his tongue was touching hers, and staying cool was the last thing on her mind. Not when her blood rushed through her body at Mach 1 and every interesting female part of her began to tingle and ache and move toward begging to be touched.

He kissed her deeply, exploring, teasing, circling. She met him stroke for stroke, wanting to arouse him as much as he aroused her. Not to prove a point, for once, but because a kiss this good should be shared. Because it felt right.

She breathed in the scent of his body. She wished she were physically capable of crawling inside of him so she could know what he was feeling at that exact moment.

Instead she tilted her head and continued to kiss him as if this had been her plan all along.

She felt the hardness of his arousal pressing into her midsection. He wanted her. There was physical proof.

It should have been a moment of rejoicing. She should have pulled away and crowed about her victory. She was more than halfway there. But while she did pull back, she didn't say a word. Instead she stared into his dark eyes, at the fire there, the fire that matched the one raging inside her.

Then she did the only thing that couldn't possibly make sense. She turned and ran.

Five

If there wasn't twenty million for charity on the line, not to mention the house itself, Jack would have been on the road back to Texas the next morning. But he was stuck for the month. All the other guys had survived their time at Hunter's Landing, so he would, too. But he would bet a lot of money that their weeks had been a whole lot less hellish than his.

He didn't want to think about his most recent kiss with Meri, but he couldn't seem to think about anything else. It had been different. He'd felt the power of his need for her all the way down to his bones. He'd ached for her in a way that was more than unsettling.

Trouble. Meri was nothing but trouble. She'd been a whole lot easier to handle when she'd been a teenager.

He walked into the kitchen, intent on coffee, only to

find one of her team members pouring a cup. Jack frowned slightly, trying to put a name with the face.

"Morning," the guy said and held out the pot for Jack.

"Morning…Colin," he added, remembering the smaller man from his arrival.

"Right." Colin pushed up his glasses and smiled. "Great house."

"I agree."

"It belongs to your friend, right? Meri's brother? The one who died."

Casual, easy words. *The one who died.* They cut through him like a razor and left wounds only he could see. "Yes. Hunter had this house built."

"Meri said this house was being turned over to the town or something. That it's going to be a place where sick people can recover and regroup. That's cool."

It was pure Hunter. Wanting to make a difference even after he was gone.

"How's the work coming?" Jack asked, not wanting to talk about his friend anymore. "Making progress?"

"Not yet. Theoretically there is a way to increase thrust within the confines of a safe formulation, but the nature of our planet seems to be that going faster and longer always means creating something toxic. Meri is determined to change that. When we consider the finite nature of our resources and the vastness of space, there are going to have to be some spectacular breakthroughs before we'll ever have a chance to explore our solar system, let alone the galaxy."

Colin took a quick gulp of his coffee. "The truth is, the next few generations are going to be like the early

Vikings. Going off on the rocket equivalent of rafts into a great unknown. If you consider their total lack of technology, the analogy is even more interesting. Because we consider ourselves cutting-edge, but compare what we have now to the first Russian launches. It's like they used paper clips and rubber bands to hold the whole thing together. But if they hadn't launched first, would Kennedy have pushed space flight? If you knew the number of modern innovations that came out of the space program..." He trailed off and looked slightly confused. "What were we talking about?"

"How your work was going."

"Oh, yeah. Sorry. I get carried away." Colin shifted slightly. "I like your car."

"Thanks." The sleek sports car wasn't practical, but it was fun to drive.

"Get good mileage with that?"

Jack grinned. "No."

"I didn't think so. I'd like a car like that."

"So buy one," Jack told him. Someone with Colin's brain had to make enough money.

"I'd like to, but it's not a good idea. I'm not a great driver." Colin shrugged. "I get easily distracted. You know, I'll be going along just fine and then I think about something with work and—zap—I'm just not paying attention. I've had a couple of accidents. I drive a Volvo. It's safer for me and the rest of the world."

"Okay, then." A sports car was not a good idea. At least Colin understood his limitations.

"Meri said you own a company that works in dangerous parts of the world," Colin said. "Interesting work?"

"More of a logistical challenge. People need to be able to work in dangerous parts of the world. My teams make sure they stay safe."

"Sounds exciting."

"It's an easy way to get dead. You have to know what you're doing."

Colin nodded slowly. He was blond and pale, with light blue eyes and a slightly unfocused expression. "Military background?" he asked.

"Special Forces."

Colin sighed. "I wanted to go to West Point. At least when I was a kid. But I was already in college by the time I was thirteen. Besides, I don't think I would have survived the physical training."

Jack had spent his six years of service staying out of any kind of officer training. "It's all a matter of discipline."

Colin smiled. "Maybe for you. For some of us there's an issue of natural ability. Or lack thereof. Meri talks about you a lot. I decided she had to be making it up, but she wasn't. You really are dynamic and powerful. Probably good with women."

Colin seemed to shrink as he spoke. Jack wasn't sure how to respond to his comments. What most interested him was the fact that Meri talked about him. Unfortunately that was the one question he couldn't ask.

"You have a thing for Meri?"

"What?" Colin's eyes widened. He pushed up his glasses again. "No. She's great, don't get me wrong, but we're just friends. She's not anyone I would...you know...be attracted to."

Jack's first instinct was to grab the little weasel by

the throat and ask him what the hell he thought was wrong with Meri. Then he got a grip and told himself to back off.

His second instinct was to walk away, because he didn't do personal conversations. But then he remembered Meri's insistence that they help Colin and Betina get together.

He refused to play matchmaker, but maybe a couple of questions couldn't hurt.

"You're a lucky guy," he said. "Surrounded by beautiful women."

Colin blinked. "Betina's beautiful."

"Yes, she is. Meri mentioned she wasn't one of the scientists?"

"Oh, no. She coordinates the project. She's just a normal person. She keeps us on track with our time and our budget. She takes care of things." His voice had a dreamy quality. "She always smells good. It's not always the same scent. Some of it is perfume, but there's an intriguing quality to her skin…."

"Sounds like someone worth getting to know."

"She is," Colin said, then paused. "What do you mean?"

"Is she seeing anyone?"

"What? I don't think so. But Betina has a lot of men. Practically a different man every week. She's always fun. I don't think the two of you would get along at all."

Jack held in a grin. "You're probably right. Have you two ever…?"

"Oh." Colin took a step back. "No. We've never dated or anything."

"Not your type either?"

"Uh, no. Probably not." But Colin sounded more resigned than anything else. As if he'd given up hope on the one thing he wanted.

Jack heard the shuttle van arriving and excused himself. He took the stairs up to his office, but as he passed the landing for the bedrooms, he paused. Meri liked to just pop into his room without warning. Maybe it was time to play the same game with her. Last night's kiss had obviously rattled her. He should press his advantage.

He crossed to her room and opened the door without knocking. Meri stood beside her bed.

The drapes were open and sunlight streamed into the room, illuminating every inch of her. Her hair fell in a wavy mass down her back. Her skin gleamed as if it had been dusted with starlight. She wore nothing but a tiny pair of bikini panties.

He stared at her nearly naked body, taking in the dip of her waist, the narrow rib cage and her perfect breasts. She held a bra in each hand, as if she'd been trying to decide which one to wear.

At last he raised his gaze to her face. She looked confused and apprehensive. There was none of her usual sass or spark.

Wanting slammed into him, nearly knocking him over with its intensity. On the heels of that came guilt. He'd promised Hunter he would keep Meredith safe from predators. Men exactly like himself.

"I'm sorry," he said and backed out of the room.

Meri dressed quickly, then stood in the center of her room, not sure what to do. Last night's kiss had been upsetting enough. She'd reacted to it with a passion that had stunned her. She'd wanted him, and nothing in her revenge plan was supposed to be about wanting.

She'd tried to convince herself that her reaction had been perfectly natural. Jack was a good-looking guy she liked a lot. She used to have a crush on him. It had been illogical to assume she could seduce him and not get aroused herself. End of story.

But she hadn't been able to totally believe herself. Now, having seen the need in his eyes, she knew the wanting wasn't all one-sided.

She left her room and went upstairs to his office. Sure enough, Jack was at his computer, staring at the screen as if it were the only thing that mattered.

"We have to talk," she said.

"No, we don't."

"I'm not leaving. You want me. I saw it in your eyes."

"I walked in on a beautiful naked woman. It was a biological reaction to a visual stimulus. Nothing more. I would have wanted anyone who fit the description."

She considered his words. Was he telling the truth? Was that all it was? Biology at work?

"I don't think so," she said. "It was more specific than that. You don't want any woman. You want me."

He finally looked up from the computer. "I've never understood why anyone would bang their head against a wall to make the pain go away, but I do now."

She smiled. "It's just part of my charm. Come on, Jack. You want me. Why can't you admit it?"

He sucked in a breath. She held hers, waiting for the words that would make her want to party like it was 1999.

"I talked to Colin about Betina," he said instead.

She sank into the chair opposite his desk. All thoughts of wanting and sex disappeared as she leaned forward eagerly. "Really? What did he say?"

"Nothing specific. You're right—he has a thing for her, but he thinks he's totally out of her league."

She groaned. "Of course he does."

"Why?" Jack asked. "He's got a lot going for him. He's smart and he has a good job. He seems nice. He should be like catnip."

"It's not that simple. Colin is like me—book-smart, world-stupid. Betina is one of those funny, social people who makes life a party wherever she goes. Colin bonds with the potted plant in the room. Trust me, I've been there."

"You were never that bad."

"I was worse. I had a wild crush on a guy I could never have. Then he broke my heart."

Jack looked out the window, then back at her. "I've apologized for that. I can't take it back."

"I know, but I like punishing you for it over and over again. The point is, being that smart isn't easy. I always knew I didn't fit in, and Colin feels the same way. We're bright enough to see the problem, but we can't seem to fix it."

"You're saying Colin can't take the steps to tell Betina he's interested?"

"He won't see himself as capable."

"Then maybe they shouldn't be together."

"I don't accept that," Meri told him. "Colin is a sweetie. And Betina is my best friend. I owe her everything. I want her to be happy. I'm going to make this happen."

"You shouldn't get involved."

"Too late. Thanks for your help."

"I didn't help."

She smiled. "You so did. When we go to their wedding, you can tell everyone how you had a hand in getting them together."

He groaned. "Or you could just shoot me now."

"Where's the fun in that?"

Six

"I have happy news," Meri told Betina that afternoon when they'd finished working for the day.

Betina glanced out the kitchen window to where the rest of the team had walked down to the water. "You're giving up your ridiculous quest to sleep with Jack?"

"Never that," Meri told her. "I'm actually getting closer by the day. He's weak with desire. I'm sure you've noticed him limping."

"You're a nut."

"Maybe, but I'm a nut with fabulous news about Colin. He likes you."

Betina had traveled the world, dated a European prince and had a very wealthy sheik invite her into his harem. She had a tattoo, knew how to do henna and had explained the intricacies of sex to Meri in such detail that her first time had been a breeze. But she'd never once, in all the years Meri had known her, blushed.

Betina ducked her head. "I don't think so."

"He does. He talked to Jack about you. He thinks you're great. He's just lacking in confidence. But you have enough confidence for two people, so you're a perfect match."

Betina raised her head. "You dragged Jack into this?"

"I didn't drag him. He wanted to help. Sort of. That's so not the point. Isn't this fabulous? Aren't you happy?"

Betina didn't look the least bit thrilled. Her friend walked over to the kitchen table and sat down. "I'm not sure I want things to change."

Meri sank down across from her. "What? Are you crazy? We're talking about Colin."

"Exactly. He's really special. Right now he's my friend and I can depend on him to always be my friend. If I change that relationship, there's no going back."

"Is that a bad thing?"

"I don't know and neither do you. Meri, there are consequences for everything we do. What if Colin and I don't hit it off? What if he's not who I think he is? Then I'll lose the friendship and have nothing."

Meri didn't understand. "I thought you were in love with him."

"I am. That's what makes this so hard. I'd rather just be his friend than not have him in my life at all."

"But you could be more. You could have it all. I don't understand. You've always been a risk taker."

"Not when something important is on the line. There I'm nothing but a coward."

This was news, Meri thought, confused by her friend. "I don't get it. You're in love with him. There's a very good chance that he's in love with you. And yet you're not going to do anything about it? You'd rather have a skinny piece of pie than the whole thing?"

"It's better than no pie."

"But if you don't try, you'll always wonder. You'll have regrets—and, believe me—those are the worst."

"How would you know?"

Meri smiled sadly. "I grew up the queen of regrets. There were so many things I wanted to do when I was growing up. But I was always afraid. I didn't fit in and I wasn't willing to risk being rejected. So I never tried. I was miserable in college, so sure no one would ever want to be my friend. Looking back, I can see a few times when people approached me. But I blew them off. It was easier to be right than to risk. But it was a high price. Like you said, there are always consequences."

"What are the consequences of sleeping with Jack?" Betina asked.

"So now we're talking about me?"

"I have more confidence in the subject."

Meri considered the question. "I finally get to move on with my life. He was my first crush and then he hurt me. I've grown up and matured, but I've never been able to let him totally go. He's always lurking in the back of my mind. If I can get over him, I can move on. He's the reason I've never been able to fall in love."

"I thought you were in love with Andrew."

Was she? Meri didn't know what real, adult love felt like. She enjoyed Andrew's company. She liked being with him. Six months ago she would have said yes, she was pretty sure she was almost in love with him. Today she was less sure.

"I haven't missed him enough," she said softly. "I've seen him only a couple of times in the past six months. Shouldn't I be destroyed without him?"

"Nothing about you is normal. Andrew seems like a good guy. You'll hook up again when you go back to D.C. You can figure out your feelings then. Assuming you're not in love with Jack."

What? "No way. I don't love him. I want to hurt him. I want to make him crawl and beg and then I want to walk away."

"That's sure the story," Betina said calmly. "The one you've been telling yourself for years. But is it the truth?" She shrugged. "I have my doubts. I think you've never gotten over Jack. I don't think any of this is about revenge. You can't accept you still love him so this is the story you tell yourself. But be careful. You're not into casual relationships. What happens if you sleep with him and then can't walk away? You want him to break your heart twice?"

In love with Jack? "Never. He can't hurt me. I won't let him. He's little more than a symbol of the issues in my childhood. Once I prove I've outgrown him, I can let my past go."

"An excellent theory. You'll have to tell me how that works out for you."

Meri hated her friend's doubts. Betina was her oracle, the keeper of social and romantic knowledge. They'd never disagreed on anything significant before.

"I have to do this," Meri said. "I've waited too long to walk away now. I have to go for it. You should, too. Tonight."

Betina laughed. "You're a brave woman. Braver than me."

"That's not true."

"It is when it comes to matters of the heart. You're willing to risk it all to get what you want, and I'm not."

Jack walked into his room that night weary from too many hours at the computer. He pulled the hem of his shirt out of his jeans and started unbuttoning it, only to stop when he heard something in the bathroom.

He turned and saw the door was closed but light shone from underneath. What the hell?

But as quickly as the question formed, it was answered. There was only one person who would be hanging out in his bathroom. Meri.

He hesitated as he tried to figure out the best way to handle the situation. With his luck, she was probably naked. Maybe in the tub. Waiting for him. She'd been doing her best to seduce him, and he hated to admit that she'd done a damn fine job. He was primed and ready. It wouldn't take much to push him over the edge.

The question was, did he want to fall?

He owed Hunter his loyalty. He'd given his word and he hadn't done much of a job of seeing it through. All his friend had asked was for him to protect his sister. Instead Jack had cut and run. Sure, he'd kept tabs on Meri from a distance, but that was taking the easy way out.

Which meant now was the time to make good on his

promise. He would walk into the bathroom, tell Meredith to get the hell out of there, explain nothing was ever going to happen between them and grit his teeth for the rest of the time he was stuck up here in the lodge.

A least it was a plan.

He sucked in a breath and walked into the bathroom.

It was as he'd expected. Candles glowing, rose petals scattered, the fire flickering and a very naked Meri in the tub.

She'd piled her hair on top of her head, exposing the sexy line of her neck. Bubbles in the bath floated across the water, giving him a quick view of her nakedness before moving to cover the scene. Her perfect breasts floated, a siren's lure calling to him.

He was hard in a heartbeat. Hard and ready to take her every way he knew how.

It wasn't her pale skin or the music playing in the background that got to him. It wasn't the way she'd set the scene or the fact that he knew she wasn't just willing, she was determined. He could have resisted all of that, even her slightly pouting lips.

What he couldn't resist was the book she was reading. She'd set out to seduce him and had gotten so caught up in a textbook on nuclear fission that she hadn't even heard him walk into the bathroom. That was the very heart of Meri. A walking, breathing genius brain trapped in the body of a centerfold. Who else could possibly appreciate the magic that was her?

Meri sighed as she turned the page. Why did Jerry have to go out of his way to make a perfectly mesmerizing topic boring? She'd been a little nervous when he'd asked her to read his latest textbook, and now that she was into it, she realized she'd been wary for a reason. Nuclear fission was one of the great discoveries of the twentieth century. Shouldn't that be celebrated? Shouldn't it at least be interesting? But noooo. Jerry wrote down to his audience and had taken what was—

The book was ripped from her hands. Meri blinked in surprise to find Jack standing beside the tub. Tub? She was in a tub? When had that happened?

She blinked again and her memory returned. Right. She'd planned on seducing him tonight. She glanced around and saw the candles and rose petals. At least she'd done a nice job.

"Hi," she said as she smiled up at Jack. "Surprise."

"You sure are that."

She braced herself for him to yell at her or stalk off or explain for the four hundredth time why this was never going to work. She didn't expect him to pull her to her feet, drag her out of the bath and haul her against him.

She was stunned. In a good way. She liked how he stared into her eyes as if she were prime rib and he were a starving man. She liked how his hands moved up and down her back, then slipped lower, to her butt.

She was totally naked. A fact he seemed to appreciate.

"But I'm all wet," she whispered.

"I hope that's true," he said before he bent his head and kissed her.

His mouth was firm and sure, claiming her with a kiss that demanded a response. She tilted her head and parted for him, wanting to get the party started with some soul-stirring kisses.

He didn't disappoint. He moved into her mouth, brushing her tongue with his, moving leisurely, as if arousing her was the only thing on his mind. Heat poured through her.

Not that she was cold. Not with the fire to her back and Jack pressing against her front.

As he kissed her over and over again, he moved his hands over her body. He touched her shoulders, her back, her hips, tracing her skin, igniting nerve endings everywhere he went.

She raised her hands to his shoulders, then slid her fingers through his hair. She touched his cheeks, feeling the stubble there, before exploring his chest.

He was strong and masculine. When he cupped her rear, she arched against him and felt the hard thickness of his erection. A thrill of anticipation shot through her. She shivered.

He pulled back a little. "Cold?"

"No."

He stared into her eyes. She stared back, wondering what he was thinking. He'd been resisting her best efforts for a while now. Did he regret giving in? Not that she was going to ask. There were some things it was best not to know.

He didn't act like a man with regrets. He bent down, but instead of kissing her lips, he pressed his mouth to her neck and nibbled his way to her collarbone.

His hands rested lightly on her waist. As he teased her neck, licked her earlobe, then gently bit down, he moved his hands up her rib cage, toward her breasts.

Before her surgery she'd been warned that she might

lose some of the sensitivity in her breasts, but she'd been one of the lucky ones. She could feel everything—every touch, every kiss, every whisper of breath. She tensed in anticipation of how Jack would make her tingle.

When he reached her curves, he cupped them gently. He explored her skin, then swept his thumbs across her nipples. Her insides tightened.

He kissed his way down to her breasts and drew her left nipple into his mouth. She leaned her head back as he circled her, then sucked and licked. Ribbons of need wove through her body, settling in her rapidly swelling center. The dull ache of arousal grew.

He turned his attentions to her other nipple, teasing and kissing until her breathing came in pants and her legs began to tremble.

Even as he continued to tease her breasts, he slipped one hand lower and lower, down her belly, toward the promised land. She parted her legs and braced herself for the impact his touch would have on her. Only he didn't touch her *there.* Instead he stroked her thighs and played with her curls. He ran his fingers along the outside but never dipped in.

She shifted impatiently, wondering if shaking him would get the message across. There! He needed to touch her *there.*

But he ignored that place where she was wet and swollen and desperately ready. He squeezed her bottom, he circled her belly button, he touched everywhere else.

Just when she was about to issue a complaint in writing, he pulled back a little, bent down and gathered her in his arms. Before she could catch her breath, he'd carried her into the bedroom and placed her on the bed. Then he was kneeling between her legs, his fingers parting her as he gave her an intimate, six-second-to-climax openmouthed kiss.

The combination of tongue and lips and breath made her moan in delight. He licked her with the leisurely confidence of a man who knows what to do and likes doing it. She gave herself over to the steady stroking and the easy exploration.

Tension invaded her. Each clench of her muscles pushed her higher and closer. One summer while she was still in college, she'd played with the idea of becoming a doctor, so she'd read several medical textbooks. She knew the biological steps leading to an orgasm—the arousal, how the blood made the area feel hot, the mechanism involved in swelling, the response of the sympathetic nervous system.

But none of those words could begin to describe what it felt like to have Jack suck on the most nerve-filled place in her body. How there seemed to be a direct connection between that engorged spot between her legs and the rest of her. How each flick of his tongue made her stomach clench and her heels dig into the bed.

She felt herself getting closer and closer. He moved patiently, slowly, drawing out the experience. Taking her to the edge, then pulling back just enough to keep her from coming.

Again and again she caught sight of her release, only to have it move out of reach.

Then, without warning, he went faster. The quick

flicks of his tongue caught her off guard. She had no time to prepare, no way to brace herself for the sudden explosion of pleasure that tore her apart.

Wave after wave of release swept through her. She pressed down, wanting to keep the feelings going. He gentled his touch but didn't pull away. Not until she experienced the last shudder and was able to finally draw in a breath.

She opened her eyes and found him looking at her. Under any other circumstance, his smug grin would have annoyed her, but considering what he'd just done, she decided he'd earned it.

She grabbed him by his shirt front and urged him to slide up next to her. When he would have spoken, she touched his mouth with her fingers, telling him to be quiet. While she loved a good relationship conversation as much as the next woman, this was a time for silence.

When he was on his back, she unbuttoned his shirt, then kissed her way down his chest to his belly. He was warm and he tasted sexy and faintly sweet. She nipped at his side, which made him both laugh and groan, then she went to work on his jeans.

He was so hard she had trouble with the zipper but finally managed to get it unfastened. He helped her push down his jeans and briefs.

She knelt between his legs, taking in the beauty that was his aroused naked body. His erection called to her. She reached out and touched him, then stroked his length. He put his hand on top of hers.

"I don't have any protection," he said.

She smiled. "Come on, Jack. It's me. When have I not prepared for every contingency?"

She leaned forward and opened his nightstand, then pulled out the condoms she'd put there before she'd started her bath.

Seconds later, the condom in place, she eased herself onto him.

He was big and thick and he filled her, stretching her inside in the most delicious way possible. She braced herself on her hands and knees, settling in for the ride.

His dark gaze met hers. "You really think I'm going to let you be on top?" he asked.

"Uh-huh."

He reached for her breasts. "You're right."

She laughed, then rocked back and forth, easing herself onto him, then off. At the same time, he cupped her breasts, teasing her nipples and providing a heck of a distraction.

She forced herself to concentrate on that place where they joined, but it got more and more difficult as her body got lost in the pleasure. With each stroke, she drove herself closer to another orgasm.

She felt him tense beneath her. She rode him faster, taking them higher and harder, pushing toward their mutual goal.

He abandoned her breasts and grabbed her hips, holding her tightly enough to control the pace. It was just slow enough to make her whimper.

So close, she thought as she concentrated on the feel of him pushing inside of her again and again. So…

And then she was coming. Her release rushed

through her, urging her on. Faster and faster until she felt him hold her still as he shuddered beneath her.

On and on their bodies joined, until they were both still.

Jack rolled her onto her side and withdrew. They stared at each other in the soft light of the room. He touched her face.

"I wasn't going to let you do that," he murmured.

"I know. You mad?"

"Not at you."

At himself? Because he'd betrayed his promise to Hunter? Meri started to tell him it didn't matter when it suddenly occurred to her that maybe it did. To him, at least. That maybe he regretted letting his friend down and that this had been the last promise he'd been able to keep.

Only he hadn't.

"Jack…" she began.

He shook his head. "Don't go there. Wherever you're going, don't."

She opened her mouth, then closed it. She didn't want to apologize. Not exactly. But she felt as if she should say something.

"I should go," she murmured

"You don't have to."

She stared into his dark eyes and knew she wanted to stay. Even if it was just one night, she wanted to spend the time with him.

"I went to a psychic once," she told him. "She told me that one day I would be in bed with the devil. I always knew she meant you. It's not your fault you gave in. It was destiny."

He smiled faintly. "You believe in psychics?"

"I believe in a lot of things. I'm very interesting."

"Yes, you are."

She sighed and snuggled close. "Are we going to make love again tonight?"

"Yes."

"You can be on top this time if you want."

He chuckled. "You're not in charge."

"Of course I am. I'm also totally irresistible. Right now you're wondering how you resisted me for so long."

"It's like you can read my mind."

She closed her eyes and breathed in the scent of him. Everything about this moment felt right, she thought. As if this was what she'd been waiting for. As if—

Wait a minute. She wasn't supposed to *like* having sex with Jack. She was supposed to be getting her revenge and moving on. They weren't supposed to connect.

They weren't, she told herself. She was just emotionally gooey from the afterglow. It was a biological response. Her body's attempt to bond with a man who was genetically desirable. Come morning, she would be totally over him and this and be ready to walk away. Her plan would go on as scheduled and she would be free to move forward with her life.

"I'm healed," Meri told Betina the next morning as she poured milk over her cereal. "Seriously, if I had a limp, it would be gone."

Betina looked her over. "Based on the smirk and the glow, I'm going to guess you and Jack did the wild thing last night."

Meri sighed with contentment. "We did. It was fabulous. Better than I imagined, which is hard to believe. I feel like a new woman. A new woman with really, really clear skin!"

Betina laughed. "Okay. Good for you."

"Any progress with Colin?"

"No. I watched a movie and he spent the evening on his computer. Then we went to bed separately."

Meri felt her fabulous mood fade a little. "That sucks. You need to talk to him."

"I'm not taking advice from you."

"Why not? My plan is working perfectly. Jack has had me and now he wants more. But he's not going to get any more. I'm walking away."

"Really?"

"Absolutely."

"And you don't feel a thing?"

"I'm a little sore," Meri said with a grin.

Betina slowly shook her head. "Okay. Then I was wrong. I guess you don't have any feelings for him. If you're not thinking about being with him again or wanting to hang out with him, then you are healed. Yay you."

Her friend poured coffee and walked out of the kitchen. Meri stared after her.

She didn't have feelings for Jack. Okay, sure, he was a friend and, as such, she would always have a soft spot for him. She was also willing to admit that not sleeping with him again might be difficult, but only because it had been so darned good. Not because she felt any kind of emotional connection.

But as she thought the words, she felt a little *ping* in her heart. One that warned her something might not be right.

"I don't care about him," she told herself. "I don't."

Which was a good thing, because falling for him would totally ruin her attempts at revenge.

She finished her cereal, rinsed the bowl and put it in the dishwasher. Then she walked into the dining room.

Someone rang the bell at the front door. She frowned. It was too early for the rest of the team, not to mention a delivery. So who on earth…?

She walked to the front of the house and opened the door. Her mind went blank as she stared at the man standing there. The man who swept her into his arms and kissed her.

"Hey, babe," he said.

She swallowed. "Andrew. This is a surprise."

Seven

When Jack finished getting dressed after his shower, he debated going downstairs for coffee or heading up to the loft to check in with his office.

Coffee won, mostly because he hadn't gotten much sleep the previous night. Sharing a bed with Meri had been anything but restful.

He walked out of his bedroom, then paused at the landing to look at the picture he'd mostly avoided since arriving at the house. It showed him and his friends during college. When everything had been easy and they'd called themselves the Seven Samurai.

Hunter laughed into the camera, because he'd always enjoyed whatever he was doing. Luke and Matt—twins who couldn't be more different—held Ryan in a headlock, while he and Devlin poured beer over the group. He knew that just outside the view of the camera sat a teenage girl on a blanket, her head buried in a book. Because Meri had never quite fit in.

Hunter had worried about her, especially after he'd found out he was dying. That's when he'd asked Jack to take care of her.

"Hell of a job," Jack muttered to himself as he turned away from the picture. Sure, Meri was all grown up now, a woman who made her own choices. That was her excuse for what had happened the previous night. What was his?

He'd wanted her. Who wouldn't? She was smart and funny and pretty as hell. She challenged him the way no one else dared. She was sexy and irreverent and so filled with life and ideas. Hunter would have been proud of her. Then he would have turned on Jack like a rabid dog and beaten the crap out of him. Or at least he would have tried. Knowing it was all his fault, Jack knew he just might have let him.

So now what? Meri had claimed she wanted to seduce him, which she probably thought she had. Did they just move on now? Pretend it hadn't happened? Because it shouldn't have, no matter how good it had been. If he could turn back time…

Jack shook his head. No point in lying to himself. If he could turn back time, he would do it all over again. Which made him a pretty big bastard and a sorry sort of friend.

He glanced back at the photo. Now what?

He heard footsteps on the stairs. But instead of a petite blonde with an attitude, he saw Betina climbing toward him.

"Morning," he said.

She reached the landing and looked at him. There was something in her eyes—something that warned him she was not happy about certain events.

"What?" he asked.

"That would be my question to you." She drew in a breath. "Look, it's not my business—"

Great. She was going to get protective. "You're right. It's *not* your business."

She glared at him. "Meredith is my friend. I care about her. I don't want her to get hurt."

"What makes you think that's going to happen?"

"It's in your nature. You're the kind of man who is used to getting what he wants and walking away."

True enough, he thought, not sure what that had to do with anything. "Meri's not in this for the long term," he said.

"That's what she keeps telling me, but I'm not so sure. I think she's in a position where she could get her heart broken."

"Not by me."

Betina rolled her eyes. "Are all men stupid about women or is it just the ones in this house?"

"You expect me to answer that?"

"No. I expect you to respect someone you're supposed to care about. You've known Meri a long time. She's not like the rest of us. She didn't grow up with a chance at being normal. She managed to fit in all on her own."

"I heard you had a part in making that happen."

Betina shrugged. "I gave her direction. She did the

work. But she's not as tough as she thinks. What she had planned for you was crazy—and I told her that, but she wouldn't listen."

"Typical."

"I know. My point is I don't want anything bad to happen to her. If you hurt her, I'll hunt you down like the dog you are and make you pay."

He gave her a half smile. "Going to hire someone to beat me up?"

"No, Jack. I'm going to tell you exactly how much she's suffering. I'm going to point out that you were her brother's best friend and that he asked only one thing of you and you couldn't seem to do it. Not then and not now. I'm going to be the voice in your head—the ugly one that never lets you rest."

He met her steady gaze with one of his own. "You're good."

"I care about her. She's part of my family. She deserves someone who loves her. Are you that guy?"

He didn't have to think about that. "No." He'd never loved anyone. He refused to care. It cost too much.

"Then leave her alone. Give her a chance with someone else."

"Someone like Andrew?" Jack had a bad feeling about him. He would get his report soon enough and then figure out what to do.

"Funny you should mention him," Betina said, looking amused. "I guess you don't know."

"Know what?"

"He's here."

* * *

Meri pulled back, stood in front of the open door and wondered if she looked as guilty as she felt. While she and Andrew had agreed that they were on a relationship hiatus, saying the words and having him show up less than four hours after she and Jack had made love for the third time of the night was a little disconcerting.

"You're here," she said, feeling stupid and awkward and really, really guilty.

"I missed you." He smiled that easy Andrew smile—the one that had first drawn her to him. The one that told the world he was pleasant, charming and curious about everything. "Did you miss me?"

She'd spent five months working on her plan to seduce Jack Howington III and nearly a week putting that plan into action. In her free time she'd been consulting for two different defense contractors and working on her solid-rocket-fuel project. Who had time to miss anyone?

"Of course," she said, resisting the urge to fold her arms over her chest and shuffle her feet.

"Good." He stepped into the house and put his arm around her. "So this is where you've been hanging out."

"I've actually been down in Los Angeles a lot. Remember? The consulting."

"I know. Is your team here?"

"They'll arrive in an hour or so."

"How fortunate." He pulled her close again. "So we have time to get reacquainted."

Ick and double ick. She couldn't get "reacquainted" with Andrew right after having seduced Jack. It was wrong on many, many levels.

She stepped away and looked at him. Andrew was tall like Jack but not as muscular or lean. His brown hair was longer, his blue eyes lighter. Jack was a sexy version of the devil come to life. He played every hand close and gave nothing away. Andrew was open and friendly. He assumed the world liked him—and most of the time it did.

Which didn't matter, she told herself. There was no need for comparisons. She had a relationship with Andrew and she had nothing with Jack. They'd been friends once, she'd proved her point and now she was moving on. She should be happy Andrew was here. He was part of the moving-on bit, wasn't he?

Andrew's blue eyes clouded. "What's wrong, Meredith? Aren't you happy to see me? It's been weeks since we met at The Symposium in Chicago. I've missed you. You said you wanted time for us both to be sure about our feelings. I'm still sure. Are you?"

Life was all about timing, Meredith thought happily as Colin walked into the room, saw Andrew and grimaced.

"Oh. You're here," he grumbled. Colin had never been a fan.

It wasn't anyone's fault, Meri told herself. Andrew was inherently athletic and Colin…wasn't. She wasn't either, but she tried and she always forced her team to attempt something new a couple of times a year. She ignored the complaints and reminded them it was good for them.

"Colin!" Andrew said cheerfully, ignoring the other man's obvious irritation at his presence. "Haven't seen you in a long time. How's it hanging?"

Colin looked Andrew over with the same enthusiasm one would use when seeing a cockroach in one's salad. "It's hanging just fine."

Colin poured his coffee and left.

"I think he's starting to like me," Andrew said in a mock whisper. "We're really communicating."

Despite everything, Meri laughed. "You're an optimist."

"Hey, you like Colin and I like you. Therefore I must like Colin. Isn't that some kind of math logic? You should appreciate that."

She should, and she mostly did. She appreciated that Andrew was never tense or intense. She enjoyed his humor, his spontaneity and how he seemed to live a charmed life. According to every women's-magazine survey she'd ever taken, Andrew was perfect for her.

So how had she been able to be apart from him for six months only seeing him for a few days at a time and not really mind?

Before she could figure out the answer, she heard more footsteps on the stairs. She turned, expecting to see Betina, who would be a great distraction. Instead Jack walked into the kitchen.

The room got so quiet Meri could actually hear her heart pumping blood through her body. She felt herself flush as she tried to figure out what on earth she was supposed to say.

Andrew stepped forward, held out his hand and smiled. "Andrew Layman. I'm Meredith's boyfriend."

Jack looked him over. "Jack Howington the third. Friend of the family."

Meri stared in surprise. Jack had used his full name, including the number. Why? He never did that.

The two men shook hands. When they separated, it seemed that they were both crowding her a little.

"So you know Meredith's dad?" Andrew asked. "You mentioned you were a friend of the family, but she hasn't mentioned you before."

"I knew her brother. Meri and I were friends in college. We go way back."

"Interesting. You never came to D.C.," Andrew said easily. "I know all of Meredith's friends there."

"Sounds like you keep a close watch on her."

"I care about her."

"Apparently not enough that you mind a six-month absence," Jack told him. "You haven't met all of Meri's friends here."

"I already know them."

"You don't know me."

"You're the past."

Jack's gaze was steady. "Not as much as you might think. Meri and I have a history together."

Meri rolled her eyes. It was as though they were a couple of dogs and she were the favorite tree they both wanted to pee on. While she was sure Jack was more than capable of winning the contest, she was surprised he would bother to play. She also hadn't expected Andrew to get drawn in. Since when had he become competitive?

"There's a little too much testosterone in here for me," she said as she stepped back. "You two boys have fun."

* * *

Meri made her way to Betina's room and found her friend typing on her laptop.

"Girl emergency," Meri said as she closed the bedroom door and sat on the edge of the bed. "How could he be here?"

"Andrew?"

Meri nodded. "I had no idea. We've been staying in touch via e-mail and we've talked a little on the phone, but there was no warning. He just showed up. How could he do that?"

"He got on a plane and flew here. It's romantic. Does it feel romantic to you?"

"I don't know," Meri admitted, still unclear how she felt. "It's been weeks and weeks. I thought he was going to propose and I thought maybe I would say yes. Shouldn't I be excited that he's here? Shouldn't I be dancing in the streets?"

"We don't have much in the way of streets, but maybe if you danced in the driveway, it would be enough."

Meri started to laugh, then sucked in a breath as she suddenly fought tears. "I'm so confused."

"You slept with Jack. That was bound to change things."

"It was supposed to make them more clear. I was supposed to be healed."

"Maybe the problem is you were never broken."

Meri nodded slowly. Maybe that *was* the problem. She'd always thought there was something wrong with her and that it could be traced back to Jack's painful rejection. But what if that had just been a normal part of growing up and, because of her freakishness, she hadn't been able to see it? What if she'd made it too big a deal?

"You don't think I needed closure with Jack?" Meri asked. "You don't think getting revenge on him will move me to a higher plane?"

Betina sighed. "I don't think anything negative like revenge is ever healthy. You've felt emotionally stalled and unable to commit. Was that about what Jack did or was it simply that you needed more time to integrate who you were with who you wanted to be? Being book-smart doesn't help you grow up any faster or better. Sometimes it just gets in the way."

"I figured that out a while ago," Meri grumbled. "You'd think I could deal with it by now." She drew in a deep breath. "I was so *sure* that revenge was the right way to go. I knew that if I could just make him want me, then walk away, I'd be happy forever."

"Maybe that's still true."

Meri wasn't sure. "Like you said—it's not healthy to be so negative."

"But it is done," Betina reminded her. "Deal with what you have now. Closure. So on to Andrew—if that's where you want to go."

An interesting idea. The only problem was Meri wasn't sure what she thought about anything anymore.

"I need to clear my head. I'm going to run. Could you get the group started without me?"

Betina grinned. "I love it when you leave me in charge."

Later that morning, Jack went looking for Meri. She wasn't in the dining room with her team, although

Betina had told him she was in the house somewhere. He checked out his bathroom, but no beautiful, naked women waited for him. Damn. There were days a guy couldn't cut a break. Then he saw something move on the balcony and stepped out to find her sitting on a chair, staring out at the view.

She looked up as he joined her. "I was going to use the telescope, but it's kind of hard to see the stars with all the sunshine getting in the way."

He glanced at the bright blue sky. "I can see where that's a problem."

"I thought about spying on our neighbors—you know, catch someone sunbathing nude. But I just can't seem to get into it."

Her big eyes were dark and troubled. The corner of her mouth drooped. She looked sad and uncomfortable, which was so far from her normal bouncy self that he found himself saying, "You want to talk about it?"

She shrugged. "I'm confused. And before you ask why, I'm not going to tell you."

"Makes it hard to help if I don't know what's wrong."

"Maybe you're the problem."

"Am I?"

She sighed. "Not really. A little, but it's mostly me."

He took the chair next to hers and stared out at the lake. It was huge, stretching for miles. "Did you know Lake Tahoe is nearly a mile deep?"

The droopy corner turned up. "Someone's been reading the chamber of commerce brochure."

"I got bored."

She looked at him. "Why aren't you married?"

The question made him shrug. "No one's ever asked."

"Oh, right. Because you're so eager to say yes?"

"Probably not. I'm not the marrying kind."

Now she smiled for real. "Sure you are. You're rich and single. What was it Jane Austen said? Something about any single man of good fortune must be in search of a wife? That's you. Don't you want to get married?"

"I never much thought about it. My work keeps me busy."

"Meaning, if you have too much time to think, you take on another job."

How had she figured that out? "Sometimes."

He liked to stay busy, involved with his business. He had some guys he hung out with occasionally. That was enough.

"No one gets close?" she asked.

"No."

"Because of Hunter?"

He stretched out his legs in front of him. "Just because we slept together doesn't mean I'm going to tell you everything I'm thinking."

"Okay. Is it because of Hunter?"

He glanced at her. "You're annoying."

"So I've been told. Do I need to ask again?"

"I should hire you to do interrogations. And, yes, some of it is because of Hunter."

"People die, Jack."

"I know. I lost my brother when he was still a kid. It changed everything."

He hadn't meant to say that, to tell her the truth. But now that he had, he found he didn't mind her knowing.

"It was like with Hunter," he said quietly. "He got sick and then he died. We'd been close and it hurt like hell that he was gone."

The difference was he hadn't kept his brother from going to the doctor. When Hunter had first noticed the dark spot on his shoulder, Jack had teased him about being a wimp for wanting to get it checked out. So Hunter had waited. What would have happened if the melanoma had been caught before it had spread?

"You didn't kill Hunter," Meri told him. "It's not your fault."

Jack stood. "I'm done here."

She moved fast and blocked the door. She was small enough that he could have easily pushed past her, but for some reason he didn't.

"You didn't kill him," she repeated. "I know that's what you think. I know you feel guilty. So what's the deal? Are you lost in the past? Are you afraid to fall for someone because you don't want to lose another person you love? Or do you think you're cursed or something?"

Both, he thought. And so much more. He wasn't allowed to love or care. It was the price he had to pay for what he'd done. Or, rather, what he hadn't done.

"I'm not having this conversation with you," he said.

"Wanna bet?"

She probably thought she looked tough, but she was small and girlie and he could take her in half a second. Or a nanosecond, to talk like her.

"Get out of my way," he growled.

She raised her chin. "Make me."

She was like a kitten spitting at a wolf. Entertaining and with no idea of the danger she was in.

"You don't scare me," he told her.

"Right back at you." Then she smiled. "But you probably want to kiss me now, huh?"

She was impossible. And, damn her, he *did* want to kiss her. He wanted to do a lot of things to her, some of which, if they stayed out here on the balcony, would violate the town's decency code.

So instead of acting, he went for the distraction. "Andrew seems nice."

"Oh, please. You hate him."

"Hate would require me thinking about him. I don't."

"So macho. What was up with the I-know-Meri-better game?"

"I have no idea what you're talking about," he said, even though he did. Establishing dominance early on was the best way to win.

"And they say women are complicated," she murmured.

Eight

Meri came downstairs and found Andrew waiting for her in the living room and her team hard at work in the dining room. The choice should be simple. Work or the man who had traveled so far to see her.

She debated, then ducked into the kitchen, found the phone book in the pantry and made a couple of quick calls.

"We're taking the afternoon off," she announced as she walked in on her team.

"Oh, good," Andrew said, coming up behind her and putting his hand on her shoulder. "Alone at last."

"Not exactly," she said with a grin. "Everyone, the shuttle will be here shortly to take you back to your hotel. I want you to put on bathing suits and beach clothes. Plenty of sunscreen."

Donny grimaced. "You're going to make us be out-doors again, aren't you?"

"Uh-huh."

There was a collection of grumbles, but everyone knew better than to argue.

"At least we'll get it over with," someone said. "Then we can work."

"You're taking them to the lake?" Andrew asked when the team had left. "Are you sure about this?"

"They can swim," she told him. "They might not be great at it, but they can. It's not healthy for us to sit in this room day after day. Being outside clears the mind. Physical activity is good for them."

He pulled her close. "You're good for me. Haven't you missed me, Meredith?"

"Yes, but maybe not as much as I should have," she told him honestly.

His blue gaze never wavered. "So I left you alone for too long. I knew I shouldn't have listened to you when you said you wanted to take a break."

"I had some things I had to do." Things she wasn't comfortable thinking about with an actual boyfriend in the wings.

She braced herself for his temper or at least a serious hissy fit. Instead he touched her cheek. "I guess I'm going to have to win you back."

Words that should have melted her heart—emotionally if not physically. Because the temperature required to melt a body part would cook it first, and that was gross, even for her twisted mind. So what was wrong with her? Why wasn't Andrew getting to her?

A question that seriously needed an answer.

* * *

An hour later they were down at the edge of the lake. Meri counted heads to make sure no one had ducked out of what she had planned and was surprised to see Jack had joined them.

"Colin told me I wouldn't want to miss it," he said when she approached.

"He's right." She had a little trouble speaking, which was weird but possibly explained by how great Jack looked in swim trunks and a T-shirt. He was tanned—mostly all over, she remembered from the previous night.

Bad memory, she told herself. Don't think about making love with Jack. Think about Andrew and how sweet he is. Although sweet Andrew had chosen not to show up for her afternoon of fun on the lake.

"So what are we doing?" Betina asked. She wore shorts and a bikini top.

Meri was momentarily distracted by amazing curves a couple of hours of surgery hadn't begun to give her. And Betina's assets were all natural.

"Um, that." Meri pointed out to the water, where four guys rode toward them on Jet Skis.

"Nerds on water," Colin muttered. "What were you thinking?"

"That you'll have fun."

"I'll get a sunburn."

Jack moved close. "I like it," he said. "Will they give them lessons?"

"Yes. And make them wear life jackets. It will be fun."

He raised his eyebrows. "Do you always bully them into some physical activity?"

"Pretty much. I'm not athletically gifted either, but I try. We can't spend out whole lives inside. It makes us pasty. This is better."

"Last year she made us ski," Colin said absently as he eyed the Jet Ski. "Norman broke his leg."

"It's true," Betina said. "To this day, the man walks with a limp."

Meri put her hands on her hips. "But he had fun. He still talks about that day, okay? We're doing this. Don't argue with me."

Jack liked the way she stood up to everyone and how they reluctantly agreed. Meri was an unlikely leader, but she was in charge.

"So where's Allen?" he asked.

"Andrew," she corrected. "He doesn't like group sports."

"Not a team player?"

"He plays tennis."

"I see."

She glared at him. "What does that mean?"

He held up both hands. "Nothing. I'm sure he has a great backhand."

"He belongs to a country club. He nearly went pro."

"Afraid of messing up his hair?"

She sniffed. "No. He wanted to do something else with his life."

"Oh. He couldn't make the tour."

"He came really close."

"I'm sure that brings him comfort."

"Look," she said, poking her finger at his chest. "We can't all be physically perfect."

He liked baiting her and allowed himself a slight smile. "You think I'm perfect."

"You're annoying. And you're not all that."

"Yes, I am."

She turned her back on him. He liked getting to her almost as much as he didn't like Andrew. Jack was still waiting on Bobbi Sue's report on the man. His gut told him it wasn't going to be good news. Would Meri listen when he told her the truth?

He refused to consider that Andrew might be an okay guy.

The instructors rode their Jet Skis to the shore. "We're looking for Meri," the tallest, tannest and blondest one said.

"I'm here." She waved. "This is my team. They're really smart but not superathletic. Sort of like me."

She grinned and the guy smiled back. He looked her up and down, then whipped off his sunglasses and moved toward her.

Jack stepped between them. He put his hand on the other guy's shoulder. "Not so fast."

Surfer dude nodded and took a step back. "Sorry, man."

"It's fine."

Meri raised her eyebrows. "You're protecting me from a guy on a Jet Ski. It's almost romantic."

"I was impressed," Betina said. "He could have carried you off to the other side of the lake. We might never have seen you again."

He eyed them both, not sure of their point.

"You overreacted," Betina said in a loud whisper. "She could have handled him herself."

"Just doing my job."

"Sure you were," Betina told him with a wink. "You're not subtle. I'll give you that."

"Didn't know I was supposed to be."

Meri sighed. "While this is lovely, let's get on with the activity. You'll take people out with you and make sure they know what they're doing before setting them loose with the moving equivalent of a power tool, right?"

"Sure thing," surfer dude said.

Jack grabbed Meri by the hand and led her over to one of the Jet Skis. "You can go with me."

"Are you being all macho and take-charge? It's un-expected—but fun."

Now she was baiting him. Which was fair, he thought as he put on a life jacket, pushed the Jet Ski back into the lake, then straddled it. If she had been anyone else, he would have thought they were a good team. But he wasn't interested in being on a team, nor was he inter-ested in Meri. Not that way.

She stepped into the lake and shrieked. "It's cold."

"Snow runoff and a mile deep. What did you expect?"

"Eighty degrees. I'll freeze."

He gunned the Jet Ski. "You'll be fine. Hop on."

She slid behind him, put her feet on the running board and wrapped her arms around his waist.

When she was settled, he twisted the accelerator and they took off across the water.

They bounced through the wake of a boat, then settled onto smoother water. Meri leaned against him, her thighs nestling him. The image of her naked, hungry and ready filled his mind. For once, he didn't push it away. He let it stay there, arousing him, making him want to pull into shallow waters and make the fantasy real.

He didn't. Instead he headed back to the beach, where her friends were being shown the right way to board a Jet Ski.

There was also a new addition to the group. A dinghy had been pulled up on the beach, and Andrew stood slightly to the side, staring at Meri.

"How about something with a little more power?" he said, pointing to the twenty-five-foot boat anchored offshore.

She climbed off the Jet Ski and pulled off her life jacket.

"I need to stay here," she told him. "This was my idea."

Andrew glanced around. "The nerd brigade will be fine." He grabbed her hand. "Come on. It'll be fun."

Jack wanted to step between them the way he had with surfer dude. But this was different. This was the guy Meri thought she wanted to marry. And until he, Jack, had proof that Andrew was only in it for her money, he couldn't do a damn thing to stop her.

"Go ahead," he told her, consciously unclenching his jaw. "I'll take care of them."

"We don't need taking care of," Colin protested, then shrugged. "Okay. Maybe we do."

Meri looked at Jack. "Are you sure?"

"Go. We'll be fine."

She nodded slowly, helped Andrew push the dinghy back into the water, then climbed on board. Andrew started the engine and then they were gone.

Colin stared after them. "I hate it when he takes her away. It's never the same without her."

Jack hated that he wanted to agree.

Meri scraped the dishes into the garbage disposal, then stacked them on the counter by the sink. She was pleasantly full from the Mexican food they'd brought in for dinner and just slightly buzzed from the margarita. Hmm, her team had had liquor twice in a week. If she wasn't careful, they were going to get wild on her.

She smiled at the idea, then caught her breath as someone came up behind her and wrapped his arms around her waist. Her first thought was that it was Jack, who'd mostly ignored her all afternoon. But then she inhaled the scent and felt the pressure of the body behind her and knew it wasn't.

"Andrew," she said as she sidestepped his embrace. "Come to help me with the dishes?"

"No. You don't need to do that. Let someone else clean up."

"I don't mind. I was gone all afternoon."

"You say that like it's a bad thing. Didn't you have fun with me?"

"Sure."

They'd taken the boat to the middle of the lake, dropped anchor and enjoyed a light lunch in the sun, then stretched out for some sunbathing. What was there not to like?

She would ignore the fact that she'd kept watching the shore to see what was going on there. To make sure her friends were all right, she reminded herself. She hadn't been looking to see if Jack stuck around. Even though he had.

"Too bad about the cabin onboard," Andrew said.

"Uh-huh."

It had been small and cramped, and when Andrew had tried to take her down below, she'd nearly thrown up. The combination of confined spaces, movement on water and her tummy wasn't a happy one.

"Let's go have more fun," he said, reaching for her hand. "Back at my hotel."

She sidestepped him. "I need to stay here."

"Why?"

"I was gone all afternoon."

"They survived. Meredith, you're not their cruise director."

"I know, but I'm responsible for them."

"Why? They're adults."

True, but they were her team. "Look, I want to stay here."

He stared into her eyes. "How am I going to win you back if you refuse to be alone with me?"

An interesting point. Did she want to be won back?

Of course she did, she told herself. This was Andrew, the man she'd thought she might marry. She'd slept with Jack; she was over him and ready to move on with her life. She could emotionally engage now. Why not with Andrew?

"I have a great suite," he told her. "With a view. If you don't want to go back to my room, we could go to a casino and go gambling. You know how you like to play blackjack."

It was true. She didn't actually count cards, but she had a great memory and there were usually only a half dozen or so decks in play at any one time. How hard could it be to keep track of three hundred and twelve cards?

Jack walked into the kitchen. He smiled pleasantly at Andrew. "You're still here?"

Andrew stepped close to her. "Trying to get rid of me?"

"I'll let Meri do that herself." He turned to her. "We're about to play Truth or Dare. I know it's your favorite. Want to join us?"

"We're going to state line to the casinos," Andrew said.

Meri glanced between the two men. They were both great in their own ways. Different but great.

"I'm tired," she told Andrew. "I'd really like to stay in tonight."

His. expression tightened. "I'm not interested in hanging out here. I'll go to the casino without you."

She touched his arm. "You don't have to do that. You could stay."

He glanced toward the dining room, where she could hear Colin arguing theoretical equations.

"No, thanks," Andrew told her. He started for the door.

She turned to Jack. "This is all your fault."

"What did I do?"

She huffed out a breath, then hurried after Andrew.

"Don't be like this," she told him on the front porch.

"Like what? Interested in spending time with you alone? I haven't seen you in weeks. The last time we talked on the phone, you said everything was fine. But now I find out it isn't. Were we taking a break, Meredith, or were you trying to break up with me? If that's what you want, just say so."

She opened her mouth, then closed it. Andrew was perfect for her in so many ways. He was exactly the man she was looking for. Added to that was the fact that she'd had him investigated and there was nothing in his past to indicate he gave a damn about her inheritance. Men like that were hard to find.

Six months ago she'd been almost sure. So what was different now?

Stupid question, she thought. Jack was different. Being with Jack was supposed to make things more clear, and it hadn't.

"I'm not trying to break up with you," she told him. "I'm glad you're here. I just need some time to get used to us being a couple."

"Hard to do when we're apart."

"So stay."

"Come back to my hotel with me, Meredith."

"I can't."

"You won't."

She wouldn't. He was right.

"Andrew…"

He walked to his car. "I'll be back, Meredith. I think you're worth fighting for. The question you need to answer is, do you want me to keep trying?"

She watched him drive away. The front door opened and Betina stepped out next to her.

"Man trouble?" her friend asked.

"When does my romantic life flow smoothly?"

"Practically never. You're always interesting, I'll grant you that. So what has his panties in a snit?"

Meri looked at her. "You never liked him. Why is that?"

"I don't mind him. I think he's too impressed with himself. But he's good to you and he passed your rigorous inspection, so that's all I need to know."

"But you don't like him."

"Do I have to?" Betina asked.

Meri shrugged. "Do you like Jack?"

"Are you doing a comparison?"

"No. I'm just curious."

Betina considered the question. "Yes, I like Jack."

"Me, too." Meri held up her hand. "Don't you dare start in on me that you knew I would fall for him, blah, blah, blah. I haven't fallen for him. It's just different now."

"What are you going to do about it?"

"Nothing. Jack and I are friends. The bigger question is, what do I want from Andrew?"

"How are you going to figure that out?"

"I haven't got a clue."

She followed Betina back inside, where everyone sat around on the oversize sofas. Two bowls filled with pieces of paper stood in the middle of the coffee table. They would be the "truth" and "dare" parts of the game.

Meri had learned not to mess with dare with this group. Not when they wanted things like mathematical proof that the universe existed. Answering personal, probably embarrassing questions was a whole lot easier.

As Jack was new to the game, they let him go first.

He pulled out a question and read it aloud. "Have you ever gone to a convention in any kind of costume?"

He frowned and turned to her. "This is as wild as you guys get?"

She laughed. "It's not a big deal for you, but—trust me—there are people in this room with guilty *Star Trek* secrets."

Jack put down the paper. "No."

Colin groaned. "You weren't supposed to get that question."

"Which means there's another one in the bowl about doing it with twins," Meri told him with a grin.

She reached into the bowl and pulled out a paper. "Have you ever been stood up?"

The room seemed to tilt slightly. She remembered being eighteen, wearing her prettiest dress, although a size eighteen on her small frame was anything but elegant. She'd had her hair done, actually put on makeup and gone to the restaurant to meet a guy from her physics lab. She'd waited for two hours and he'd never shown up.

The next day he'd acted as if nothing had happened. She'd never had the courage to ask if he'd forgotten or done it on purpose or for sport.

Jack leaned over and grabbed the paper from her. "She's not answering the question. This is a stupid game."

"I don't mind," she told him.

"I do. I'll tell them about the twins."

All the guys leaned forward. "For real?" Robert asked. "Twins?"

She shook her head. "Jack, it's okay."

"It's not. What happened is private."

What happened? How could he know she'd been stood up? He'd been gone for months. Actually, the nondate had gotten her to think about changing. She'd joined a gym the next day.

She started to tell him that, then found she couldn't speak. Her throat was all closed, as if she had a cold…or was going to cry. What was wrong with her?

"Excuse me," she said and ducked out of the room. She hurried into the kitchen to get a glass of water.

It was stress, she told herself. There was too much going on.

She heard footsteps and turned to find Colin entering the room.

"You okay?" he asked. "I'm sorry about the question. It wasn't for you. I was hoping Betina would get it."

Something inside Meri snapped. "I've had it with you," she said. "Look, you're a grown single man interested in a woman who obviously thinks you're hot. For heaven's sake, do something about it."

He opened his mouth, then closed it. "I can't."

"Then you don't deserve her."

Nine

Meri needed coffee more than she needed air. It had been another long night but not for any fun reasons. She'd tossed and turned, not sure what to do with her life—something she hadn't wrestled with in years.

She was supposed to have things together by now. She was supposed to know her heart as well as she knew her head. Or did being so damned smart mean she was destined to be stupid in other ways?

The coffee had barely begun to pour through the filter when someone rang the doorbell. She hadn't seen anyone else up yet so she walked to the front door and opened it.

Andrew stood on the porch. He held a single red rose in one hand and a stuffed bright-green monkey in the other.

"It's possible I behaved badly yesterday," he said

with a shrug. "More than possible. I want things to work between us."

She didn't know what to say. While she was relieved to not be fighting, she wasn't exactly in the mood to throw herself into his arms. Which meant that there was a whole lot more for them to deal with.

"Andrew, this is really confusing for me," she said. "You're right. We were apart too long. Things have changed."

"Is there someone else?"

"No," she said without thinking, then had to wonder if that was true.

Not Jack, she told herself. Okay, yes, they'd gotten intimate, but just the one time and nothing since. He was her past. The problem was Andrew might not be her future.

He handed her the monkey. "I brought you this. I thought it would make you smile."

She took the ridiculous stuffed toy. "He's adorable. What about the rose?"

"That's for me. I plan to wear it in my teeth."

He bit down on the stem, which made her laugh. Andrew always made her laugh. Wasn't that a good thing? Shouldn't she want to be with him?

"You want some coffee?" she asked. "I have a pot going."

"Sure." He took a step inside, then grimaced as his cell phone rang. "Sorry. I'm dealing with some stuff at work. Give me ten minutes?"

She nodded and stepped inside. Still carrying the monkey, she returned to the kitchen. Only this time she wasn't alone. Colin stood pouring coffee. He wore jeans, an unbuttoned shirt and nothing else. But it wasn't his unusual outfit that got her attention. Instead there was something about the way he stood. Something in the tilt of his head or the set of his shoulders.

"Colin?"

He turned and smiled at her. "Morning."

A single word but in a voice she'd never heard from him. It was low and confident. He was a man at peace with himself and the universe.

She felt her mouth drop open. "You had sex with Betina."

Colin didn't even blush. "It wasn't sex, Meri. It was making love. And, yes, we did. She's amazing. She's the woman I've been waiting for all my life."

With that, he collected two cups of coffee and carried them back to his room.

Meri laughed out loud. She set the monkey on the counter, then turned to find someone to share the good news with.

But she was alone in the kitchen, so she ran upstairs, taking them two at a time, then burst into Jack's office. He was on the phone but hung up when he saw her.

"You look happy," he said. "So it's not bad news."

"I know. It's fabulous. I saw Colin. He's someone completely different. He and Betina slept together and I think they're seriously in love. Isn't that fabulous? Are you jazzed?"

One corner of Jack's mouth turned up. "Good for Colin. I didn't think he had it in him."

"Oh, there was a tiger lurking behind those silly plaid shirts. And we're a part of it. We got them together."

Jack held up his hands in the shape of a T. "There's no 'we' in all this. They got themselves together."

"Don't be silly. We pushed. And I mean *we*. You were a part of it. You acted like a matchmaker. I'm so proud."

He groaned. "Leave me out of it."

She crossed to the window, then turned back to face him. "This is great. They may get married. We can go hang out at the wedding and take all the credit."

"I don't think so."

She wrinkled her nose. "You're not getting in the spirit of this. It's happy news."

She spun in a circle, holding her arms out and tilting back her head. Soon the room was turning and turning. She lost her balance and started to fall. Which should have worried her, except Jack was there to catch her.

She collapsed against him, then smiled up into his face. He had the most amazing eyes, she thought absently, then she dropped her gaze to his mouth. That part of him wasn't so bad either.

"You need to slow down," he told her.

"No way. Light speed isn't fast enough."

"You'll get hurt."

What were they talking about? She found she didn't know and she sort of didn't care. Not as long as he held her.

"Jack," she breathed.

He released her and stepped back. "Meri, this isn't a good idea."

Then it hit her. She'd run to Jack instead of Andrew.

That couldn't be good. Had Betina been right all along? Had there been more on the line that getting revenge or closure or any of the other reasons she'd given herself for wanting to sleep with Jack? Dear God, what had she done?

"I have to go," she whispered and hurried out of the room. She ran all the way to her bedroom, then closed the door behind her and leaned against it. Where did she go from here?

Jack poured coffee. As he raised his mug, Colin walked into the kitchen.

Meri was right—there was something different about the guy. An air of confidence. He wasn't just a nerd anymore.

The love of a good woman, Jack thought humorously. Apparently the old saying about it being able to transform a man was true. Lucky for him, he'd escaped.

"How's it going?" Colin asked.

"Good. With you?"

"Great."

"No one seems to be talking trash in the dining room today," Jack said.

"Meri gave us the day off."

Probably to ensure that Betina and Colin spent more time together. It was just like her.

"Andrew was here before," Colin said.

"What happened?"

"Something with his office. He had to leave."

"You sound relieved."

Colin shrugged. "He's not my favorite."

"Mine either."

They were an interesting group, these scientists, Jack thought. Brilliant and humble, funny, determined and willing to make fools of themselves on Jet Skis. They looked out for Meri. Hunter would have liked them a lot.

"What?" Colin asked. "You have a strange look on your face."

"I was thinking about Meri's brother. He would have liked you. All of you."

"Meri talks about him. He sounds like a great guy."

"He was. A group of us became friends in college. We called ourselves the Seven Samurai. It was dumb but meaningful to us. Hunter was the connection we all had with each other. He brought us together. Held us together."

Then he'd died and they'd drifted apart.

Jack thought about his friends—something he didn't usually allow himself to do—and wondered how they'd enjoyed their months in Hunter's house. Had their worlds been flipped around and changed or had the weeks passed quietly?

"It's good to have friends like that," Colin said. "Meri's a lot like him. She draws people together. Gets them involved. She handpicked the team for this project. They let her do that because she's so brilliant."

Jack nodded. Meri's brain was never in question. "She's more outgoing than she used to be."

"She's grown up. It's hard for us, the freaks." Colin grinned. "That's what she calls us and herself. We all had to deal with not fitting in and stuff. Meri wants us to put that aside and deal with life as it is. Look forward. That sort of thing."

There was affection in his voice, but not the romantic

kind, so Jack didn't have to kill him. He realized that the reports might have told him the specifics but they hadn't allowed him to get to know the woman she'd become.

"I was thinking about your business," Colin said. "There's some new military software that could help with your security issues."

"Military software? Is it classified?"

Colin grinned. "Sure, but I know the guy who wrote it. There's a couple of beta versions floating around. I might be able to get you a copy to test out—you know, as a service to your government."

"Lucky me." Jack eyed the other man. "You're a lot more dangerous than you look."

Colin grinned. "I know.

"Left foot green," Betina called.

Meri looked down at the Twister sheet on the floor and groaned. "I'm not built to bend that way."

"The very reason I don't try to play the game. But so not the point."

"You're basically mean," Meri muttered. "I don't know why I didn't see that before. Sorry, Robert. I'm going to have to slide under you."

Robert arched his back as best he could. "Good luck with that. You do realize you're in danger of hyperextending your shoulder."

Colin looked up from his awkward position. "I'm not sure she would hyperextend it. Technically speaking—"

"Stop!" Meri yelled. "I don't want any technical talk right now. Let's pretend to be normal."

Colin and Robert both frowned at her. "Why?"

She started laughing, which made bending and stretching impossible. But she still tried, because the big green dot was just out of—

She wobbled, leaned, then collapsed, bringing everyone down with her. She landed on Robert, and Colin sank down on top of her.

"I'm not sure I approve of this," Betina said from the sidelines. "Colin, do we need to talk about fidelity?"

"Not really." He grunted as he rolled off Meri, then scrambled to his feet. "Unless you want to spank me."

Meri gagged. "I so did not want to know that about you two."

"I'm surprised," Robert said from his place on the floor. "Usually men who enjoy domination have powerful positions in their work life. It's an attempt to obtain balance and let someone else take responsibility."

Meri looked at him. "Is there anything you don't know?"

"How to get the girl. Any girl."

"We'll talk later," Meri said, offering her hand and helping him to his feet. "I'm on a roll. Are you interested in anyone in particular?"

Before he could answer, Jack walked into the room. There was something about his expression that warned Meri he didn't have good news.

"What's wrong?" she asked. "Is someone hurt?"

"No, but we need to talk."

He took her arm and led her into the kitchen. She didn't like anything about this.

After folding her arms over her chest she said, "So talk."

His dark eyes were unreadable. "Andrew isn't who you think."

She'd thought maybe her father had been in an accident or had a heart attack. But Andrew?

"Not who I think? You mean like secretly a woman?"

"I'm serious, Meri. I have some information on him. His background. He's not the man he's pretending to be. He's in it for the money."

A thousand different thoughts flashed through her brain. At any other time she would have paused to marvel at the exquisite structure of the human mind—of how it could hold so many contradictory ideas at any single moment. But right now all she cared about was being strong enough to punch Jack in the stomach.

"What the hell are you going on about?" she asked, her voice low and cold. "Why would you know anything about Andrew?"

"I had him investigated."

Anger burned hot and bright. "You have no right to get involved in my personal life. Who do you think you are?"

"I know you're upset—"

"Upset? You have no idea. Dammit, Jack, this is wrong on so many levels." She glanced toward the door to the living room and lowered her voice. "Just because we slept together doesn't mean you get to tell me what to do. You gave up that right the day you walked out on me after Hunter died. You were supposed to be there for me and you weren't. So I don't care what you think about anything."

She started to walk away. He grabbed her arm and held her in place.

"You have to listen to me," he said.

"No, I don't. Not that it matters, but I already had Andrew investigated. Thoroughly. He's clean. He comes from a comfortable background. He doesn't have my trust fund, but he's not hurting for money. He's a good man."

"He's married."

Her entire body went cold. She knew intellectually that her core temperature was what it had been five seconds ago, but the sensation of being on the verge of turning to ice was incredibly real.

"You're wrong," she breathed. "My investigator—"

"Did exactly what I did the first time I learned about Andrew. A basic investigation. That's usually good enough. But when you said you were thinking of marrying this guy, I had my people dig deeper. It was eight years ago. They hooked up and conned an old man out of about two million dollars. Three years ago, they took another heiress for the same amount. I'm guessing you were their next target."

She couldn't deal with the news about Andrew, so she turned on Jack. "You dug into his background? What gives you the right?"

"Someone has to look out for you. Your father is useless. With Hunter gone, there was only me." His gaze was steady. "I couldn't do what Hunter asked—I couldn't stay in your life. I was too destroyed by what had happened. Still, I had a responsibility to look out for you. So I did. From a distance."

"You spied on me?"

"Call it what you want. I made sure you didn't get into trouble."

He'd paid people to watch her? To poke into her private life? But he'd never cared enough to get involved himself?

"Bastard," she breathed and raised her hand to slap him.

He grabbed her by the wrist and held her still. "It was for your own good."

"That's a load of crap. You were trying to assuage your guilt by doing the least you could. You weren't a good friend to my brother and you sure as hell weren't a friend to me. You don't get to do this, Jack. You aren't running my life. I'll marry Andrew if I want and you can't stop me."

"Bigamy is illegal in all fifty states."

Andrew—married? She couldn't believe it. He might not be the handsome prince she'd first imagined, but married?

"He's not playing me," she insisted even as she wondered if he was.

"How do you know? At least look at the report. Then make your own decision."

There was nothing to look at, she thought sadly as she pulled her hand free of his grip. Nothing to consider. She wasn't in love with Andrew. She'd been fighting that truth since he'd shown up here. Their time apart had demonstrated that big-time. She hadn't missed him.

Had she ever been in love with him? Did it matter? If he was married and playing her, then he was nothing but a weasel.

"Your gender sucks," she muttered.

"I agree."

"You most of all. I will never forgive you for spying on me. For spending the last eleven years hiding in the shadows."

"I cared about what happened to you."

"Is that what you call it? I would say you were nothing more than a coward trying to quiet a ghost. But I know my brother. I know Hunter would never stop haunting you. He expected more, Jack. And so did I."

Ten

Meri lay on her bed facedown, fighting tears. Betina sat next to her, lightly rubbing her back.

"I can't believe it," Meri said into her pillow. "I can't believe he did that."

Betina patted her shoulder. "*I* can't believe I have to ask, but who are we talking about? Andrew or Jack?"

"Both of them," Meri muttered, then rolled onto her back and wiped away her tears. "That's my current life. I have two men betraying me."

She could say the words, but she didn't believe them. She couldn't believe any of this. How had everything gone so wrong?

Betina sighed. "I'm shocked by what Jack found out about Andrew. Do you believe him?"

Meri nodded. "He wouldn't lie about that. He said

Andrew and his wife had a whole scam going. I'm not sure what his plan was with me. He couldn't have married me, and I wouldn't have given him money for anything."

Although, now that she thought about it, he had mentioned a few investment opportunities right before she'd left.

Her stomach hurt from all the emotional churning.

"I thought about marrying him," she admitted. "When I found the ring, I knew he was going to propose and I thought about saying yes."

"You didn't."

"He didn't ask. I don't know what would have happened. Maybe he was planning to propose, then tell me I had to pay off his wife so he could get a divorce." She shuddered. "It's awful. I slept with him. I slept with a married man. I would never do that."

"You didn't know. He tricked you. You're the innocent party in all this."

Meri didn't feel very innocent. She felt dirty and gross and confused.

"I liked him," she said. "I don't know if I ever really loved Andrew, but I liked him. Shouldn't I have known? Shouldn't I have sensed something wasn't right?"

Betina shook her head. "Why? He set out to deceive you. You're a decent person who accepts people for who and what they are. You did a regular background check on him and it came back clean."

"I'm never using that investigation agency again," Meri said. "I wonder if Andrew found out the name of the guy and bought him off."

"Very possibly."

"I hate Andrew."

"No, you don't."

Meri wiped away more tears. "I don't. I can't care enough about him to hate him. I feel disgusted and I'm sick that I let myself get played. That's what hurts about him. That he used me and I was too stupid to recognize what was going on. I hate being stupid."

"No one is smart all the time. Meri, it's awful. It sucks big-time. But here's the thing—you escaped Andrew relatively unscathed. Nothing bad happened. The only thing hurt is your pride, and not even very much at that."

Meri knew her friend was right. Still, memories of all the time she spent with Andrew flashed through her head.

"I introduced him to my friends. You guys never liked him. I should have paid attention to that."

"We have amazing insight. What can I say?"

Meri started to laugh, but the sound turned into a sob. She rolled onto her side.

"Jack was spying on me. He watched me from a distance. He never cared enough to even take me to lunch, damn him. How could he do that? It's gross and creepy."

It was more than that. It was painful to think that Jack would keep his word to Hunter enough to pay others to keep tabs on her but that he didn't care enough to do it himself.

"He was wrong to act like that," Betina said soothingly.

Meri raised his head. "You're going to defend him, aren't you? You're going to say he did the best he could with what he had. You're going to say he was hurting, too, that he blamed himself for Hunter's death. He does, you know. Blame himself. Hunter had melanoma. He saw this weird black thing on his shoulder and wanted to go to the doctor. Jack teased him about being a girl and worrying about nothing."

"That can't be easy to live with."

Meri sniffed. "Statistically, getting the diagnosis a few weeks earlier wouldn't have made any difference in the end. Hunter was going to die. Not that Jack would care about that. He would still blame himself, because that's who he is."

"I don't have to defend him," Betina told her. "You're doing it for me."

"I'm not. He's a low-life who cared only about himself. I was totally alone. My mother was dead, my father is possibly the most emotionally useless man on the planet. I was seventeen. I had no one. No friends, no family to speak of. I was alone in the world and he abandoned me."

"He should have stayed," Betina said. "He should have stayed and taken care of you. I wonder why he didn't."

"Guilt," Meri said with a sigh. "Guilt about Hunter and maybe guilt about me. About how he handled things." Betina knew all about Meri's pathetic attempt to seduce Jack years ago and how badly he'd reacted.

"He was twenty-one and nowhere near grown-up enough to be responsible for a seventeen-year-old with a crush on him. So he left and I had to deal on my own."

"You did a hell of a job," her friend told her. "Hunter would be proud."

Meri considered that. "He wouldn't like my plan to get revenge on Jack."

"Brothers rarely enjoy thinking about their sisters having sex with anyone."

That made Meri almost smile. "You don't approve of it either."

"I don't approve one way or the other. I'm worried about you. I think you wanted to sleep with Jack for a lot of reasons, and none of them have anything to do with punishing him."

"You think I'm still in love with him."

"It would explain a lot."

Meri rolled onto her back and stared up at the ceiling. In love with Jack. Was it possible? The way her personal life was going, it made sense. He'd spent the last ten years doing the least he could justify when it came to her, and she might have spent the same amount of time desperate to give her heart to him.

Jack was staring at his computer screen when Colin walked into his office.

"What's up?" he asked.

"You hurt Meri," Colin said. "That's not right. You can't be so insensitive that you wouldn't know how much the information about Andrew would bother her. Not to mention the fact that someone she respected and thought of as a friend had been spying on her."

"You're not telling me anything I don't already know," Jack told him.

Colin moved closer to the desk. "That's not good enough."

Was Colin trying to intimidate him? Jack didn't think it was possible, but Colin was a changed man since his night with Betina.

"She had to learn the truth about Andrew. She said

things were getting serious. Andrew could have taken her for a lot of money."

"It's not about the money," Colin told him. "It's about trust and caring and being there for someone. She expected more of you, and you let her down."

Small words. Unimportant words, yet they made their point, Jack thought grimly.

"I was trying to protect her," he said, knowing it wasn't enough of an answer.

"There were a lot of different ways to do that. Did you have to pick one that hurt?"

"How the hell was I supposed to tell her the truth about Andrew without hurting her?"

"I'm not talking about Andrew."

Jack nodded slowly. "You're right. I should have thought through telling her that I'd been keeping an eye on her. I did it for her own good."

"No one believes that. You did what was easy, and that's not allowed. You can't go around hurting people like that. It's wrong. Meri matters to me, and I'm going to protect her—even from you."

Jack stood. He was a good half head taller than Colin and about thirty pounds of muscle heavier. He wanted to tell himself that Colin's threats were pitiful. The man couldn't hurt him if he were armed and Jack was unconscious. But he was oddly touched by Colin's bravery in the face of certain defeat. The man took care of the people who mattered, no matter what it might cost him personally.

"It wasn't my intention to hurt Meri," Jack said slowly. "But I'm going to have to do it again."

Colin narrowed his gaze. "What do you mean?"

"I'm going to make Andrew go away."

Colin nodded slowly. "I'd like to be there when that happens."

Andrew's hotel room overlooked the lake. All the right trappings were there—the computer, the lobbying magazines. He looked the part and he played it well. He'd fooled a lot of people.

"This is a surprise," Andrew said as he held open the door, a tacit invitation to Jack and Colin. "To what do I owe this honor?"

"I'm here to run you out of town," Jack said, his voice calm and pleasant. "Colin's going to watch."

Nothing about Andrew's expression changed. "I have no idea what you're talking about."

"Sure you do. I don't know how you passed the preliminary background check. Maybe you're that good at covering your tracks. You might have paid off Meri's investigator, although you couldn't have paid off mine. So I'll give you credit for creating a good front."

Andrew sat on the sofa across from the small fireplace. He waved at the two chairs opposite.

"I'll stand," Jack said.

"Me, too," Colin told him.

"As you prefer," Andrew said. "I have to tell you, this is all fascinating. So what do you think you've found out about me?"

"That you're married. That you and your wife con people for money. You know Meri is worth nearly a billion dollars. She must have been a hell of a prize for the two of you."

Andrew's expression never changed. "I have no idea what you're talking about. I've never been married."

"I have copies of the certificate in the car. Do I have to send Colin to get it? I also have the police statements from the people you two duped. Lucky for you, you didn't break any actual laws. It's not a crime to be stupid."

"You have me confused with someone else," Andrew said calmly. "I care about Meredith. We've been dating for a long time. The relationship is serious. As for your ridiculous claims, ask her yourself. I've never once talked to her about money."

"It was all just a matter of time until you did. Or it would have been."

Andrew was a pro—Jack would give him credit for that. But he was still a rat rooting in garbage.

"It's all just your word against mine," Andrew said. "I'm assuming you told Meredith all this?"

Jack nodded.

"She won't believe you."

"You sound confident," Jack said. "Funny she hasn't phoned you."

"She will."

Would she? Was she mad enough at Jack to want to get back with Andrew? How far would she take things?

He didn't have an answer, so he did the only thing he could think of to protect her.

"How much?" he asked. "Give me a number."

Andrew smiled. "You want to pay me off."

"If that's what it takes. How much?"

The other man hesitated, and in that moment Jack knew he'd been right. If Andrew had been who he claimed, he would have refused any payment.

"Ten million," Andrew said. "Ten million and I'll sign anything you want."

"Five million and you'll still sign."

Andrew smiled. "Done."

Twenty minutes later Jack and Colin were back in Jack's car.

"You paid him off," Colin said. "I thought you'd just beat the crap out of him and be done with it."

"That would have been my preference. But he's good at what he does. He could have gone back to Meri and convinced her I was the jerk in all this. This way, she'll never want him back. He can't ever hurt her."

He had a copy of the check he'd written to Andrew, along with a signed letter saying Andrew was freely taking the money in exchange for never seeing Meri again. Just to be safe, Jack had insisted on a thumbprint under the signature.

"So it's done," Colin said. "She's safe."

"It's not done," Jack told him. "Now I have to tell her what happened."

The house was quiet when they returned. Colin disappeared downstairs, probably to fill Betina in on what had happened. The nerd brigade hadn't shown up for work, which had probably been previously arranged to give Meri some time alone. Better for him, he thought.

He walked up the stairs to the bedroom level and

walked to her closed door. After knocking, he pushed it open.

She'd pulled a chair over to the window. She sat curled up in the chair, staring out at the lake.

"Go away," she said without looking at him.

"How do you know I'm not Betina or Colin?"

"I recognized your footsteps."

"Not my 'foul stench?'"

She turned to look at him. Her face was pale, her eyes red and swollen. "Don't you dare quote *Star Wars* to me, Jack. You haven't the right."

She was hurt. He could see it, but worse, he could feel it. Her pain was a tangible creature in the room. It didn't attack him. Instead it lived and breathed, reminding him that he'd let her down…again.

"We have to talk," he told her.

"No, thanks. I have nothing to say to you."

"That's okay. I'll do the talking. You just listen."

She shrugged, then turned her head back so she was facing the window. He didn't know if she was looking out or not. He had a feeling she was crying, which made him feel like crap.

"Andrew's gone," he said.

"Let me guess. You bought him off."

"I didn't trust him to leave any other way."

"And you didn't trust me to be able to resist him? Do you think he's that charming or that I'm that weak?"

"You're pissed at me. I didn't know how far you'd go to punish me."

She drew her knees to her chest. "I wouldn't give myself to a man who lied to me or tried to play me. You're not worth that."

"I wasn't sure."

"How much?"

He could have lied. He could have said there wasn't money involved. But he wanted to be honest with her.

"Five million."

She didn't react. "I'll have my accountant send you a check."

"You don't need to pay me back. I wanted to keep you safe. That's what I've always wanted."

"Because of your promise to Hunter?"

"Yes."

"But not because of me."

He didn't know what she was asking so he couldn't respond. She looked at him again.

"How many others have you paid off?" she asked. "How many other times have you gotten involved in my life?"

"Twice before."

She sucked in a breath. "The ones who just disappeared? Who broke up with me for no reason?"

"I guess. I wasn't involved in the details."

She stood and faced him. "Of course not. Why would you bother when you have a staff? It must have been desperately uncomfortable to be so close now. Distance makes things tidy. You don't have to deal with emotion."

She put both her hands flat on his chest and shoved him hard. He didn't move.

"Damn you," she cried. "I hate this. Do you know how

much I hate this? I wasn't even a person to you. I was a project. You couldn't be bothered to get involved yourself."

"It wasn't like that. I wanted you to be safe. I didn't want you with the wrong guy."

"And you know who that is?"

"Yes."

She dropped her arms to her sides, then stared up at him with tears in her eyes. "So who's the right guy? Or does he exist?"

"I don't know."

"It's not you."

She wasn't asking a question, but he answered it anyway. "No. I'm not him."

"Just the devil?"

"I'm not that bad."

"You are to me," she said and turned away. "You shouldn't have done it, Jack. It's a zero-sum game. All or nothing. You can't hide in the middle. Hunter would be disappointed, and so am I. It would have been better to just disappear. At least that would have been honest. I could have respected that."

"I don't need your respect," he said, then realized that maybe he did. For some reason, Meri's opinion mattered. As did Hunter's.

He started to leave, then paused at the door. "I didn't know how to be there for you, Meri. I didn't know how to look at you from across Hunter's grave and tell you I was sorry. I didn't know how to be what you needed. So, yeah, I left. But you were never alone. I was always looking out for you."

"That wasn't much consolation when I sat by myself

in a dorm room on Christmas Eve, with nowhere else to go," she said. "And it was more than feeling guilty about Hunter's death. You hated that I had a crush on you."

He thought about that afternoon when she'd turned seventeen and had cried her heart out.

"I didn't know how to help. I couldn't be the guy you wanted me to be."

Her mouth twisted. "Tell the truth, Jack. You couldn't stand me because I was fat and ugly."

Her pain had grown until it threatened to suck all the air out of the room. He felt it and ached for her. He'd always had a rule of never letting anyone get close. Never letting anyone see the truth about him—not the emptiness of his heart or the darkness of his soul.

He walked over and grabbed her arms, forcing her to face him. "Did it occur to you that I liked you a lot? That I saw the woman you would become and knew that I would never measure up? Did you ever once think that by letting Hunter down I knew I'd lost both of you forever?"

Tears filled her eyes. "Don't be cruel. Don't pretend I mattered."

"You did matter. We were friends. Could there have been more as you'd gotten older? I always thought so. Until it was impossible because of what I'd done. I let him down. I let you down. I knew it and I couldn't face either of you."

He turned away and walked to the door. "I lied to you before. About Hunter. I think about him every damn day."

He reached for the door handle but instead felt something warm. Somehow Meri had gotten in front of him. She touched his face, his shoulders, his chest.

"Jack, you have to let it go. You didn't do anything wrong. Hunter would never want you to suffer like this."

"I don't know how else to make it right," he admitted.

"So you're going to punish yourself forever?"

He nodded slowly.

"You're right," she whispered. "I am the bright one in this relationship." Then she leaned in and kissed him.

He told himself to resist. That being with her was the last thing he had the right to do. But her mouth was soft and insistent, and her hands urged him forward. She was beautiful and caring and sexy and smart. How was he supposed to resist her?

She touched her tongue to his bottom lip, then nipped at his flesh. Fire shot through him. Fire and need and the knowledge that for a few minutes he could forget the past and live only in the present.

"You're a hard man to convince," she murmured as she grabbed his hand and placed it on her breast.

He caressed the curve. "But at least I'm hard."

Eleven

Meri laughed softly as Jack swept her into his arms, then carried her to the bed. He set her down, bent over her and kissed her with a hot need that made her want to forget everything but the moment, the man and how he made her feel.

His mouth was firm, his tongue insistent. He touched her everywhere, his hands tugging at clothing, pulling it off until she was naked. He stroked her body, caressing her bare skin, arousing her with a quick touch of her breast, fingers teasing the curve of her hip, dipping between her legs, then moving away.

It was like being attacked by a sensual, marauding beast who took what he wanted in sneak attacks. A tickle at the back of her thighs, a quick lick on her nipple, a puff of hot breath against her neck. Over and over he touched her, then moved on before she could get lost in the moment.

She writhed beneath him for several minutes, alternately laughing, then moaning. She finally drew him to a stop by wrapping her legs around his hips and holding him in place on top of her.

He braced himself above her, his dark eyes bright with passion, his mouth tempting.

"You're playing with me," she murmured.

One corner of his mouth turned up. "Tell me you don't like it."

"I can't."

"Meredith."

He breathed her name like a prayer. The sound caught her off guard, seeping inside of her, making her strain toward him. But for what? Sexual release? Or something far more dangerous?

Before she could decide, he bent down and kissed her. She parted for him, welcoming the stroke of his tongue and the arousal his touch brought. She reached between them and tugged at his shirt. She unfastened the buttons and he shrugged it off.

His jeans went next, and his briefs. He'd walked in barefoot. When he was as naked as she, he leaned toward her nightstand and opened the drawer. The condoms she'd bought were under the book she'd been reading.

But instead of putting one on, he dropped the protection on the corner of the nightstand, then shifted onto his side. He bent down and took her right breast in his mouth, at the same time reaching between her thighs to tease the most sensitive part of her.

She parted her legs and tried to catch her breath as he explored her swollen center, then dipped inside. He mimicked the act of love with his fingers before easing up to that one important spot and circling it.

He rubbed her gently, then harder and faster. He moved so he was kissing her mouth, even as he continued to touch her there. Around and around, taking her higher with each stroke, keeping ahead of her somehow, so she was the one chasing him. Chasing the sensations that made her body tense and promised a release that would shatter her world.

She tried to catch her breath, but there was a tightness in her chest that made it hard to breathe. The closer she got, the more her heart seemed to squeeze until, as she reached the point of no return, the pain gave way.

She shattered, both inside and out. Her orgasm claimed her in a rush that erased every thought in her head but one: she loved Jack.

Through the waves of pleasure, that single truth grew until she wondered how she'd ever convinced herself otherwise. Of course she loved him. She'd loved him from the first moment she'd met him and for all the eleven years they'd been apart. She'd never loved anyone else.

Her body slowed and relaxed, but not her mind. Not even when he put on the condom, then eased between her legs and filled her until she knew she was going to come again.

He made love to her with a steady rhythm designed to spin her into madness, and she went willingly, wanting to get lost in the sensation.

But the feel of his body on hers wasn't enough to clear her mind. Nor were the waves of release, the heat, the sound of his gasps for air or the pounding of *his* heart.

Meri clung to him for as long as he would let her, holding him close, wanting time to stand still. If only she could believe that was possible. But it wasn't. She knew enough about the universe to know all things were in motion—at their most basic level. That nothing was static.

Which meant, in time, with luck, her pain would fade. Because the other thing she knew down to the cellular level was that Jack would never love her back.

Jack breathed in the scent of Meri's body as he stroked her face. She was so beautiful. She'd always been beautiful.

He slid off her so he wouldn't snap a rib, then propped his head up on his hand and wondered what the hell he was supposed to say. What happened now?

She sat up and reached for her clothes.

"Where are you going?" he asked. "An appointment?"

He smiled as he spoke, but when she looked at him, his smile faded. There was something wrong—he could see it in her blue eyes.

"What?" he asked.

"I have to go."

"Where?"

"Away. We both know this is not what you want or need. You've never been the guy to settle down. I don't know if you can't or you won't. Some of it is your guilt over Hunter and some of it is…honestly I don't have a clue what it is."

She blinked several times, then swallowed. "I can't stay with you, Jack."

He hadn't thought about her leaving until she said she had to, and now he didn't want her to go.

She scrambled out of the bed and pulled on her clothes. "This is crazy. All of it. I don't know what I was thinking. I had this great plan. Betina warned me, but did I listen? And I'm supposed to be the smart one."

"What are you talking about?"

She slid on her T-shirt, then looked at him. "You have to stop it, Jack. You're not allowed to spy on me anymore. I know you'd call it looking after me. Whatever it is, you have to stop. I'm a grown woman and I can take care of myself. If there are mistakes to be made, then I'll make them. Stop protecting me."

"I don't want to."

"This isn't about you."

He didn't understand. They'd just made love. It had been great. So why was she leaving? And when the hell had it gotten so cold in this room?

"Just like that?" he asked, getting angry because it was easy and something he could understand.

She slipped her feet into her sandals. "Just like that. Goodbye, Jack."

Then she was gone.

He stared at the door. What was going on? What had just happened? She couldn't leave. Not like this.

He swore, then scooped up his clothes and put them on. He had no idea what she wanted that she hadn't gotten. Was she still pissed about Andrew? About the fact that he, Jack, had watched out for her?

She should be grateful, he told himself as he stalked up the stairs to his office. He'd taken care of her. He'd kept her safe. That had to be worth something. She was just too stubborn to admit it.

Still angry, he opened his computer and did his damnedest to get lost in work. It was the only safe place he could think to go.

Meri burst into Betina's room without knocking. It was only after she heard scrambling that she realized she might have interrupted something.

"I'm sorry," she said, turning away. She hadn't seen anything—the tears had blinded her.

"Wait," Betina said. "You don't have to go."

"I'm in the way."

"You're not."

Her friend grabbed her and pulled her close. Meri went willingly, needing the support. She had a vague impression of her friend in a robe and a guy hovering in the background, then the tears began again.

"What happened?" Betina asked as she stroked Meri's hair. "What did Jack say?"

"Nothing. He didn't have to. I get it. I've been so stupid. You were right about everything. I didn't want revenge or closure. I'm in love with him. I have been for years. He's the reason I can't seem to commit to any-one else. I love him. I was afraid to admit that, so I came here with my crazy idea of showing him. I think I secretly thought he'd take one look at the new and improved me and be struck by lightning or something."

Meri sank onto the floor and let the tears flow. She

hurt so much. It felt as if someone had cracked open her chest and ripped out her heart.

"How can I be so smart and so stupid at the same time?" she asked.

"Because you're human and no one is smart when it comes to matters of the heart."

Made sense, she thought, wishing it were a year from now and the pain had lessened. Not that she expected it ever to go away. She had a bad feeling she would love Jack forever.

"He doesn't want me," she whispered. "He never did. I thought it was about the age difference or how I looked, but now I'm not so sure. I think maybe it was just me."

Which made it hurt. She couldn't change who she was any more than she already had. He didn't want the very essence of her being. What else was left?

"He's an idiot," Betina murmured.

"No. He's just a man who can't pretend to be in love with me." Meri sucked in a breath. "I have to go. I can't stay here. We'll need to regroup somewhere else. Maybe down south. Pasadena or something."

"Don't worry about it. Do you want me to go with you?"

Meri managed a smile as she looked at her friend. "No. I want you to stay with Colin and be in love for the both of us."

Jack worked until dark. When he finally realized he couldn't see anything other than his computer screen anymore, he stood and stretched. It was only then he noticed the silence of the house.

Uneasiness slipped through him as he went downstairs and pushed open the door to Meri's room.

The furniture was exactly as he remembered—with the exception of the bed. Someone had stripped off the sheets and left the blankets neatly folded. The closet was empty, as were the drawers. She was gone.

He raced down to the main floor, where he found Betina packing up the notes from the dining room.

"What are you doing?" he demanded.

"Leaving." She didn't bother to look at him.

"All of you?"

She nodded. "We'll finish the work elsewhere."

Work? He didn't care about the work. He cared about Meri. "Where is she? She can't leave. She has to stay the month."

He'd known that from the beginning. That she was stuck here, too. Just like him. They couldn't escape each other. Hadn't that been the point?

Betina looked at him. "She doesn't have to stay here. That was just something she told you. Hunter's donation has nothing to do with her. It was always about his friends."

She'd lied about having to stay? Why? So he wouldn't force her to leave? To make him think he had time?

"Where is she?" he asked again.

"I'm not going to tell you. If she wants you to know, she'll get in touch with you herself."

He didn't understand any of this. Why had Meri been here in the first place? What had she wanted? Why leave now?

"Is it Andrew?" he asked. "Is she upset because I told her what he was?"

Betina's expression was almost pitying. "It's a guy thing, right? This failure to comprehend the most basic of human emotions? It has to be. I can't believe you're honestly that stupid." She smiled, then shook her head. "It always comes down to smart and stupid. How strange."

"What are you talking about?"

"Nothing," she told him. "Meri came here because she thought she wanted closure. She got it, in a way. She's been in love with you all these years. But the man wasn't really you. He was someone better. The person she thought you would be. Meri embraces life. She loves and is loved. She cares about people. She thought you were all those things, too. But she was wrong. And now she's gone."

Meri loved him? She couldn't. Not after what he'd done. Not after he'd let her down time after time.

"She can't," he whispered.

"That's what I keep telling her, but does she listen?" Betina closed the box. "I'm done here. Colin and I will be gone within the hour. Then you can have the house to yourself. You've got a few weeks left, right? I hope you enjoy your time here."

She started to leave. He grabbed her arm. "You can't leave it like that. There has to be more."

"Why? You don't want there to be more. It's not like you really care about her. She's just Hunter's little sister, right? An annoying responsibility. Your problem is you didn't know what you had until you lost it, and now she's gone forever. Goodbye, Jack."

He released her and let her go because there was nothing left to say.

Fine. He could be fine his last few weeks here. It was just three weeks, and then he'd go back to Texas and bury himself in his work. He would stay busy and he would forget. He was good at forgetting.

Three days later, Jack knew he was damn close to slipping into madness. The house was empty. Too empty. The silence mocked him. Worse, he found himself missing Meri's nerd friends. He missed the arguments about string theory and the scraps of paper with equations that had dotted every surface. He missed walking into a room and not understanding a word of what was being said despite the fact that everyone was speaking English.

He missed the closeness, the way Meri bullied everyone to get outside, to live life. He missed her insisting on a better telescope because the stars were so beautiful. He missed the sound of her voice, her laughter, the way her body moved. He missed her quirky sense of humor, her brilliance and how her smile could light up a room. He missed *her.*

She wasn't the teenager he'd known all those years ago. The young woman who had intrigued him and at the same time scared the hell out of him. Not just because she was Hunter's sister but because there was a quality about her that warned him she would expect only the best of herself and those in her world.

For a while he'd thought maybe he could live up to those expectations, but then Hunter had gotten sick and he'd known he would only hold her back.

He'd let her go for a thousand reasons that made

sense at the time. She didn't need him. She had to grow up on her own. She was better off without him. He was afraid. They'd both been so young and his feelings for Meri had been confused. So he'd walked away and stayed away. He'd kept tabs on her from a distance. He'd taken the coward's way out.

He hadn't expected to ever see her again. Then she'd been here and he'd been thrown. She'd wanted to seduce him and he knew he couldn't let that happen. Because of what he owed both her and Hunter.

He walked into the empty living room and stared at the perfectly arranged furniture. It was all so comfortable. He wanted to throw things, break things, mess it all up. Because life wasn't tidy or comfortable. It was a pain in the ass.

He turned to leave, then spotted a DVD case on the floor, by the sofa. Someone had dropped it. Or left it on purpose. Meri? Betina? Hunter?

He picked it up and stared at the plain black cover. Someone had stuck on a piece of paper covered with a single word.

Hunter.

Against his better judgment, Jack walked to the DVD player and put in the disk. Then he turned on the television and braced himself for the pain.

Someone had taken the time to transfer Hunter's home movies, he thought as he watched snippets of the first confusing days at Harvard. There were shots of Hunter's friends. All of them. And Meri. She was always hanging on the fringes.

She'd been the one to show them around, list the

best places to get pizza at three in the morning. She'd been there since she was a kid.

There were shots of snowball fights and a late-night party by a bonfire.

He leaned back against the sofa and lost himself in the images. A vacation here, a camping trip there. Seven guys who had become friends. No. Brothers. Brothers he hadn't seen or talked to in years.

The scene shifted to a yacht vacation they'd all taken one spring break. The camera panned to show the guys stretched out in the sun after a very late night. Meri walked on deck and paused, looking awkward and unhappy. She turned her gaze to him. He had his eyes closed and didn't see the look on her face. The one that clearly showed she loved him.

He felt it then, the cold slice of pain that was almost familiar. It took him a second to place it and then he remembered the knife attack in a Central American jungle. At first there had been nothing—just a breath of expectation, followed by the warm sensation of liquid as his blood flowed out. Then there had been the sharp sting that had quickly grown into agony.

It was the same today. As if razors had sliced his heart and his soul, as he realized he'd lost something precious. Something he could never replace.

He picked up his cell phone and pressed the buttons that connected him to his office.

"I don't have anything," Bobbi Sue snapped by way of greeting. "If you'd stop calling me, I might get a chance to find her."

"She has to be somewhere."

"You think I don't know that? She turned in the rental car at the airport in Los Angeles, but she didn't get on a plane. If she's in a hotel somewhere, she's using cash and a false name. I'm checking all her friends to see if they've used their names to register her. It's taking time."

He didn't have time. He had to find her *now*. He'd spent every minute of the past three days thinking he had to go after her himself, but leaving meant blowing the donation, and Meri would hate him for that.

"Keep looking," he said and hung up. To give his assistant the time she needed.

Jack stood and paced the length of the living room. He wanted to be doing the search himself, but he was trapped in this damn house. Trapped with memories and ghosts and a burning need he'd acknowledged three days too late.

He loved her. He had for a long time. In college, he'd assumed she would grow up and they'd get together. The plan had existed in the back of his mind, as if he'd known they were meant for each other. Then Hunter had died and everything had changed.

His cell rang. He reached for it.

"You found her?"

"I'm not looking for her."

The voice was familiar. "Colin?"

"Uh-huh. So you're looking for Meri?"

"I have my entire staff on it."

"You won't figure it out. Besides, what does it matter?"

"It matters more than anything."

"I *want* to believe you."

Because Colin had information. Why wouldn't he?

Meri would tell Betina where she was going and Betina would tell Colin.

"I have to find her," Jack said hoarsely. "I love her."

"What if that's too little too late?"

"I'll convince her."

There was an excruciating minute of silence.

"I kind of believe you," Colin said. "Okay. When your month is up there, I'll tell you where she is."

"What?" Jack roared. "You'll tell me now."

"Sorry. No. You have to stay. It's a lot of money on the line."

"I'll pay them the difference myself."

"Okay, yeah. You're probably good for it. But leaving now violates the spirit of what Hunter was trying to do. You really think Meri will be happy about that?"

"You think she's happy thinking I don't care about her?"

"Good point, but I'm not going to tell you. Not until the time is up."

The call ended. Jack picked up the coffee table and threw it through the sliding glass door. The glass shattered with a satisfyingly destructive sound.

"Dammit all to hell," he yelled into the subsequent silence.

And no one answered.

Twelve

Meri was thinking maybe she should get a dog. One of those small ones she could travel with. From her corner room at the Ritz-Carlton in Pasadena she could see down into a beautiful grassy area, with plants and paths where people walked their small dogs several times a day. At least then there would be something else alive in the room with her.

She glanced at her watch, then sighed. Her team wouldn't arrive for another half hour, which meant time to kill. Maybe it was just her, but the days had gotten much longer in the past few weeks. The things she loved no longer made her as happy as they once had. She found it more difficult to laugh and sleep and be really excited about Colin and Betina's announcement that they were getting married.

Not that she wasn't thrilled for her friends. There was nothing she wanted more than their happiness. It was just...

She missed Jack. Yes, that was crazy and made her an idiot, but there it was. She missed him—his voice, his touch, his laugh. The way he took charge and wasn't the least bit intimidated by her. She'd loved him most of her life. How was she supposed to stop loving him?

"Therapy," she murmured as she continued to stare out the window. It had helped her before—to figure out what normal was. Maybe talking with a paid professional could help her get over Jack. Maybe she could find a really cute male therapist and do a little emotional transference, because getting over anyone else had to be so much easier than getting over Jack.

She closed her eyes against the pain. He would be gone by now. His month at Hunter's house had ended at midnight. Had he already started back to Texas or was he just getting on the road? What was he thinking of her? Would she ever be the one who got away or was that just wishful thinking on her part? She knew he would come back for the reunion, but for now, he was gone.

There was a knock at the door. Housekeeping, she thought. Okay. That was fine. They could clean while she walked the grounds and made friends with the little dogs. Maybe an owner or two could give her some advice on which kind to get.

Jack would be a big-dog kind of guy, she thought absently. Of course, if she had his feelings to consider, she wouldn't need a dog in the first place. She would have a husband and a family, although a dog would be nice, too. Maybe one of—

She opened the door and stood staring. "You're not housekeeping."

Jack pushed past her into the room and shrugged. "I can go get you more towels if you need them."

"I don't need towels."

She stared at him, unable to believe he was here. He looked good—tired and maybe thinner but still powerful and sexy and the man of her dreams.

"You're supposed to be heading home," she said. "Your four weeks are up."

He looked at her. "Is that what you think? That I'd put in my time, then walk away?"

"Sure."

"Because it's what I've always done. Put in my time, kept my distance, not gotten involved."

Her stomach flipped over a couple of times. Okay, physically it couldn't turn, but the churning caused by anxiety did a really great imitation.

She wanted to throw herself into his arms. She wanted him to hold her and tell her it was going to be all right. Only he wouldn't, because nothing in her life had ever been that easy. She had no idea why he was here. Maybe to offer her some advice or something. She would smile politely, listen, push him out the door, then have a private breakdown. She was getting good at those.

"How did you find me?" she asked.

"Colin told me."

"What? He didn't."

"Oh, yeah. But he did it in a way you can totally

respect. He tortured me first. He called right after you left and said he knew where you were but he wasn't going to tell me until my month was up. Something about a donation and that damn house."

Colin had called Jack? She wasn't sure if she should be happy or planning to return the engagement present she'd already bought.

"You were looking for me?" she asked cautiously.

Jack touched her face. "What do you think?"

"I don't know."

"You must have had an idea. You went to a lot of trouble to stay hidden."

"I don't want your pity," she admitted. "I don't want you watching over me anymore. I don't want to be a project or Hunter's little sister."

His eyes were dark and unreadable. Something flashed through them.

"Would you settle for being the woman I love?"

She heard the words. The vibration of sound worked its way through her ears and was transmitted through her brain via—

"What?" she asked, suddenly not caring about the hows and whys of her body. "What?"

"I love you, Meri. I have for a long time. I always thought…" He shrugged. "I thought there was something between us back then. But you were young and I was young and then Hunter got sick. I couldn't deal, so I ran. You know all this. I ran, but I couldn't let go. I took the coward's way out. I spied on you. You were right to call it that. I kept track from a distance, where it was safe. Where I was safe."

She had to sit down. Her legs felt weak and the room was spinning. Instead she reached for him, and he caught her and held her as if he might never let go.

"I missed you," he murmured, speaking into her hair. "I missed you so much. Not just the past three weeks, although they were hell, but for the past eleven years. I'm sorry I didn't know before. I love you, Meri. I want to be with you. I want to make this right."

He grabbed her by her upper arms and held her in front of him. "Can you forgive me? Can you tell me what to do to make it right? Can you ever care about me?"

She began to laugh and cry and went back into his arms, where he held her so tight she couldn't breathe.

It felt good. It felt right.

"Of course I love you," she said, her voice shaking. "What did you think all this was about?"

"You're a complicated woman. I had no idea. You left. That confused me."

"I wanted to leave before you could dump me. I couldn't have my heart broken again."

"I'll never leave you," he promised. "I love you. I want to be with you always. Marry me?"

It was as if someone had injected fizz into her blood. She felt light and bubbly and more happy than she'd ever been.

"What kind of dogs do you like?" she asked.

"Whichever ones makes you happy."

She smiled. "Good answer."

The first time Hunter Palmer had gone into the light, he hadn't known what to expect. Until he'd been diagnosed and told he had weeks to live, he'd never thought about having a soul or what it meant to die. Now, ten years later, he had all the answers. But there were still questions. Questions only his friends could answer.

He moved through the reception celebrating the dedication of Hunter's House, unseen, unfelt but very much there—for his friends. Once they had been the Seven Samurai—men who had vowed friendship forever. After he'd died, they'd gotten lost. Now they'd found their way back.

Hunter moved close to Nathan Barrister.

Six months ago Nathan had never heard of Hunter's Landing. Now he was married to Keira, the mayor of Hunter's Landing, and dividing his time between a house in Knightsbridge, London, and Keira's house here in the mountains.

His life was rich and full and more than he could have ever imagined. And he owed it all to Hunter. All of them did. Nathan closed his eyes and whispered his thanks to the friend who had somehow made all of this possible. And somehow he was sure Hunter heard him.

"What're you smiling about?" Keira asked, leaning into his shoulder, tipping her face up to his.

"You," he said, wrapping his arm around her and holding on tightly. "I'm smiling because of you."

"Ooh, that's what I like to hear." She turned to look at the remaining Samurai and the women who had saved them—loved them. "It's a wonderful day. I think your friend Hunter would have approved."

"Are you kidding? He would have loved this. All of us together again. Whole again." With Keira in his arms,

Nathan looked out at his friends and the women who had become the heart of the Samurai. They weren't the same, any of them. Somehow, through the magic of this place, they'd all become *more*. Smiling down at his wife, Nathan said, "I just don't think it's possible to be any happier than I am at this moment."

"Wanna bet? I have a surprise for you," she said, wrapping her arms around his middle and staring up into his eyes. "And I think today is the perfect day for this announcement."

"Yeah?" He looked at her and thought about the coming night, when he could hold her close in their bed, lose himself in the wonder of loving and being loved. "I love a good surprise."

"We're going to have a baby."

"We're what?"

"You're going to be a daddy."

"When?" His heart jolted, then kicked into a gallop. "How? What?"

"Surprise!"

She looked so happy. So beautiful. And she'd given him everything.

"I love you," he said, cupping her face between his palms. "Thanks for loving me back."

"My pleasure. Believe me."

He did. He believed her. Just as he believed that his life, his world, was only going to get better and better. Holding on to his wife, he tipped his head back, looked to heaven and said again, "Thanks, Hunter. I really owe you for this."

Hunter touched his friend's shoulder and moved on…to Luke.

It was just the kind of event Hunter would have enjoyed, Luke thought. Plenty of cold beer, good food and beautiful girls.

Make that beautiful *women*. Their time in the house had brought each of the remaining Samurai a lover with whom the men intended to spend the rest of their lives. Hunter couldn't have known that would happen…or could he?

Luke grinned at his fanciful thought, then caught Lauren's eye. "Hey, do you think we'll have time later for a round or two at the Game Palace?"

"Pool during the reunion?" She twisted one of her blond curls around her finger.

"Why not? We'll invite Matt and Kendall along and we can kick their butts. How much do you want to bet she's never played?"

Lauren frowned. "I thought you were giving up your competitive ways."

Luke snagged her in one arm and drew her close. "You know that won't happen. I've just learned to temper them with a little perspective. And with a lotta love from you, honey."

"And from Matt."

Luke gazed over the top of her head at his twin brother, who looked equally relaxed and equally loved by his Kendall. He and Matt had spent a lot of their lives as each other's enemies, but their time at Hunter's House had resolved their conflicts and returned them to a brotherhood that Luke appreciated more each day.

From across the room Matt looked up as if he'd heard

Luke's thoughts. Like many twins, they could communicate without a sound. His brother lifted his sweating beer in a little toast, and Luke returned it. Then he directed another toast heavenward.

Thank you, Hunter. I vow to live a better, fuller life.

Then he looked back down at the woman who owned his heart. "Speaking of vows…"

She tilted her head. "What?"

"A little birdie told me that a couple in this room is planning on sneaking off to Reno on Sunday to tie the knot."

"Really?"

He nodded, then captured her left hand so he could rub his thumb over the engagement ring he'd placed there. Yes, he was living a better, fuller life, but oh, how he still enjoyed winning. "Now, if we make a quick dash tonight, my sweet, sweet Lauren, we could just beat them to the altar…."

Hunter laughed quietly as he moved away. Luke would never change. Of course, Lauren didn't want him to, which was why they were so happy together.

He looked around the room and saw Devlin Campbell looking uncharacteristically worried.

As happy as Devlin was to see his old friends, he was more anxious to get home. Nicole's obstetrician had forbidden her to travel by plane with the baby so close to being born, and he missed her.

Ryan wandered over, Devlin's best man and the same guy who had declared he was swearing off women for the month he was to be at the lodge. But the Love Shack had weaved its magic on Ryan as it had the rest of them. He'd found true love, too.

"What's right with this picture?" Devlin asked Ryan as they glanced around the room.

Ryan smiled. "Yeah. Amazing. And you're missing Nicole, I'll bet."

"As much as I've liked getting together with all the Samurai, I want to be home."

"Think we'll do this again sometime? A gathering of the clan?"

"We should. Maybe a golf weekend somewhere once a year."

"It would take some doing, coordinating our schedules."

"One thing I've learned, Ryan—you have to make time for what's important. My wife, the Samurai. You're important."

"Let's go propose the idea while the wives are around to hear. They'll force the issue. Women like that kind of bonding stuff."

As if on cue, Devlin's cell phone rang. Panic struck him full force when he saw it was Nicole. Had she gone into labor without him?

"You okay?" he asked.

"I love you. I miss you. That's all."

He relaxed. She loved him and missed him. *That's all.* Such an elemental part of his life now. His beautiful wife, her love and devotion. But *that's all?*

On second thought, maybe it *was* that simple. Maybe that was the secret of life. The best things weren't complicated.

Hunter nodded. He touched Devlin's arm to ease his worry. Nicole would be fine. Then he followed Ryan across the room.

His arm draped around Kelly's shoulders, Ryan looked around at the Seven Samurai who'd finally gathered together again. He said *seven* because he knew Hunter was here in spirit. In fact, Hunter had brought about this reunion, thanks to his will.

Hunter had always been the glue that had bound them together, and now they were his legacy.

Ryan looked down at Kelly. They'd been married just weeks, but they'd been the best damn weeks he'd had in a long time. Since before his mother and Hunter had died, in fact. He felt alive again.

They'd gotten married in an intimate ceremony in California's Napa Valley. Erica and Greg had served as the matron of honor and best man. Because it was summer break, he'd been able to fly them in, along with their kids, for a family vacation. He grinned thinking about how thrilled Kelly's friends had been to get away to a romantic place, even if it was with the kids in tow.

He and Kelly would be in the same situation in a few years, especially if they kept having the same steamy nights they'd been having the past few weeks.

Kelly glanced up at him. "Why are you grinning?"

He bent and murmured something sinful in her ear.

She went still, looked embarrassed, then swatted him playfully. "Behave."

He laughed as he straightened because she'd given him exactly the reaction he would have predicted.

"Impossible with you, Venus," he responded irrepressibly.

Hunter chuckled, patted his friend on the back, then walked toward Luke's twin.

It was strange, Matthias thought, seeing all six of them together again after so many years. Even stranger that they were here without Hunter. Though, in a way, maybe Hunter *was* here with them. Maybe he'd been with them all along. And it was fitting that Hunter had been the one to bring them all together again, since he'd been the one who'd united them in college. They were still the Seven Samurai, Matthias supposed, but now one was missing. And somehow the Six Samurai just didn't seem right.

Then he realized they weren't six anymore. They were twelve. And they weren't Samurai anymore, either. Samurai were warriors, always prepared for death. Matthias, Luke, Ryan, Jack, Nathan and Devlin were family men now, focused on their lives ahead with the women who had made them complete.

That was what Kendall had done for him, anyway. Completed him. Filled in all the empty places that he hadn't wanted to admit were empty.

As if she'd sensed something, Kendall looked up at him, narrowing her gaze thoughtfully. "What are you thinking about?" she asked. "You look…happy."

"That's what I'm thinking about."

"Not the Perkins contract?"

"Nope."

"Not the Endicott merger?"

"No."

"Not the Sacramento conference?"

He tightened his fingers around hers. "I'm thinking about our life together. And I'm thinking about how we need to get right to work on that."

"You're the boss."

He shook his head. "No. We're a newly announced partnership. One that's going to take the world by storm."

She pushed herself up on tiptoe and brushed her lips over his. "I'll prepare the memo at once."

"We'd better make it a PowerPoint demonstration," he told her. "This is going to be big."

Hunter nodded with pleasure. Everything had turned out the way he'd hoped. The possibilities had been there, of course, but his friends had been the ones to take the right steps.

Last he turned to Meri, his sister. He'd missed her, but he was proud of the woman she'd become. It had taken her and Jack far too long to find each other, but at last they had.

He eased close, wishing he could hug her and tell her how much he loved them both.

"There's something about the house," Meri told Jack. "All these people falling in love. It's almost scary."

"You scared to be in love with me?"

She smiled. "Never. I'm used to it. I've loved you a lot longer than you've loved me."

"Have not."

"Have to."

Jack grinned. "Are all our fights going to be this mature?"

"I hope so." She leaned close to him. "I love you,

Jack. I think Hunter would be very happy to know we're together."

Jack nodded. "I agree. I know it's strange, but there's a part of me that thinks he wanted this all along."

If Hunter had eyes to roll, he would have done it. Then he cuffed his friend on the shoulder. What else would he have been talking about when he'd made Jack promise to take care of his sister?

It had all worked out in the end. For each of his friends. When he'd known he was dying, he'd vowed to find some way to make sure they stayed together—brothers. He'd been afraid that guilt and time and distance would pull them apart. On a sleepless night weeks before his death, the idea of the house had been born.

Now, ten years later, he was content. His sister was finally where she belonged and his brothers had become the men he knew they could be. He would tell them everything…eventually.

He smiled at them. His work here was done. He would wait for them on the other side, in a better place than they could begin to imagine. Hunter turned then, moving into the light…this time to stay.

* * * * *

Welcome to cowboy country...

Turn the page for a sneak preview of
TEXAS BABY
by
Kathleen O'Brien
An exciting new title from Harlequin Superromance
for everyone
who loves stories about the West.

Harlequin Superromance—
Where life and love weave together in emotional and
unforgettable ways.

CHAPTER ONE

CHASE TRANSFERRED his gaze to the road and identified a foreign spot on the horizon. A car. Almost half a mile away, where the straight, tree-lined drive met the public road. He could tell it was coming too fast, but judging the speed of a vehicle moving straight toward you was tricky.

It wasn't until it was about two hundred yards away that he realized the driver must be drunk...or crazy. Or both.

The guy was going maybe sixty. On a private drive, out here in ranch country, where kids or horses or tractors or stupid chickens might come darting out any minute, that was criminal. Chase straightened from his comfortable slouch and waved his hands.

"Slow down, you fool," he called out. He took the porch steps quickly and began walking fast down the driveway.

The car veered oddly, from one lane to another, then

up onto the slight rise of the thick green spring grass. It just barely missed the fence.

"Slow down, damn it!"

He couldn't see the driver, and he didn't recognize this automobile. It was small and old, and couldn't have cost much even when it was new. It was probably white, but now it needed either a wash or a new paint job or both.

"Damn it, what's wrong with you?"

At the last minute, he had to jump away, because the idiot behind the wheel clearly wasn't going to turn to avoid a collision. He couldn't believe it. The car kept coming, finally slowing a little, but it was too late.

Still going about thirty miles an hour, it slammed into the large, white-brick pillar that marked the front boundaries of the house. The pillar wasn't going to give an inch, so the car had to. The front end folded up like a paper fan.

It seemed to take forever for the car to settle, as if the trauma happened in slow motion, reverberating from the front to the back of the car in ripples of destruction. The front windshield suddenly seemed to ice over with lethal bits of glassy frost. Then the side windows exploded.

The front driver's door wrenched open, as if the car wanted to expel its contents. Metal buckled hideously. Small pieces, like hubcaps and mirrors, skipped and ricocheted insanely across the oyster-shell driveway.

Finally, everything was still. Into the silence, a plume of steam shot up like a geyser, smelling of rust and heat. Its snake-like hiss almost smothered the low, agonized moan of the driver.

Chase's anger had disappeared. He didn't feel anything but a dull sense of disbelief. Things like this didn't happen in real life. Not in his life. Maybe the sun had actually put him to sleep….

But he was already kneeling beside the car. The driver was a woman. The frosty glass-ice of the windshield was dotted with small flecks of blood. She must have hit it with her head, because just below her hairline a red liquid was seeping out. He touched it. He tried to wipe it away before it reached her eyebrow, though, of course that made no sense at all. Her eyes were shut.

Was she conscious? Did he dare move her? Her dress was covered in glass, and the metal of the car was sticking out lethally in all the wrong places.

Then he remembered, with an intense relief, that every good medical man in the county was here, just behind the house, drinking his champagne. He found his phone and paged Trent.

The woman moaned again.

Alive, then. Thank God for that.

He saw Trent coming toward him, starting out at a lope, but quickly switching to a full run.

"Get Dr. Marchant," Chase called. "Don't bother with 9-1-1."

Trent didn't take long to assess the situation. A fraction of a second, and he began pulling out his cell phone and running toward the house.

The yelling seemed to have roused the woman. She opened her eyes. They were blue and clouded with pain and confusion.

"Chase," she said.

His breath stalled. His head pulled back. "What?"

Her only answer was another moan, and he wondered if he had imagined the word. He reached around her and put his arm behind her shoulders. She was tiny. Probably petite by nature, but surely way too thin. He could feel her shoulder blades pushing against her skin, as fragile as the wishbone in a turkey.

She seemed to have passed out, so he put his other arm under her knees and lifted her out. He tried to avoid the jagged metal, but her skirt caught on a piece and the tearing sound seemed to wake her again.

"No," she said. "Please."

"I'm just trying to help," he said. "It's going to be all right."

She seemed profoundly distressed. She wriggled in his arms, and she was so weak, like a broken bird. It made him feel too big and brutish. And intrusive. As if touching her this way, his bare hands against the warm skin behind her knees, were somehow a transgression.

He wished he could be more delicate. But he smelled gasoline, and he knew it wasn't safe to leave her here.

Finally he heard the sound of voices, as guests began to run around the side of the house, alerted by Trent. Dr. Marchant was at the front, racing toward them as if he were forty instead of seventy. Susannah was right behind him, her green dress floating around her trim legs.

"Please," the woman in his arms murmured again. She looked at him, the expression in her blue eyes lost and bewildered. He wondered if she might be on drugs. Hitting her head on the windshield might account for this unfocused, glazed look, but it couldn't explain the crazy driving.

"Please, put me down. Susannah… The wedding…"

Chase's arms tightened instinctively, and he froze in his tracks. She whimpered, and he realized he might be hurting her. "Say that again?"

"The wedding. I have to stop it."

* * * * *

Be sure to look for TEXAS BABY,
available September 11, 2007,
as well as other fantastic Superromance titles
available in September.

REQUEST YOUR FREE BOOKS!

2 FREE NOVELS PLUS 2 FREE GIFTS!

Passionate, Powerful, Provocative!

YES! Please send me 2 FREE Silhouette Desire® novels and my 2 FREE gifts. After receiving them, if I don't wish to receive any more books, I can return the shipping statement marked "cancel." If I don't cancel, I will receive 6 brand-new novels every month and be billed just $3.80 per book in the U.S., or $4.47 per book in Canada, plus 25¢ shipping and handling per book and applicable taxes, if any*. That's a savings of almost 15% off the cover price! I understand that accepting the 2 free books and gifts places me under no obligation to buy anything. I can always return a shipment and cancel at any time. Even if I never buy another book from Silhouette, the two free books and gifts are mine to keep forever.

225 SDN EEXJ 326 SDN EEXU

Name	(PLEASE PRINT)	
Address		Apt.
City	State/Prov.	Zip/Postal Code

Signature (if under 18, a parent or guardian must sign)

Mail to the **Silhouette Reader Service™:**
IN U.S.A.: P.O. Box 1867, Buffalo, NY 14240-1867
IN CANADA: P.O. Box 609, Fort Erie, Ontario L2A 5X3

Not valid to current Silhouette Desire subscribers.

Want to try two free books from another line?
Call 1-800-873-8635 or visit www.morefreebooks.com.

* Terms and prices subject to change without notice. NY residents add applicable sales tax. Canadian residents will be charged applicable provincial taxes and GST. This offer is limited to one order per household. All orders subject to approval. Credit or debit balances in a customer's account(s) may be offset by any other outstanding balance owed by or to the customer. Please allow 4 to 6 weeks for delivery.

Your Privacy: Silhouette is committed to protecting your privacy. Our Privacy Policy is available online at www.eHarlequin.com or upon request from the Reader Service. From time to time we make our lists of customers available to reputable firms who may have a product or service of interest to you. If you would prefer we not share your name and address, please check here. ☐

SDES07

**Don't miss the first book in the
BILLIONAIRE HEIRS trilogy**

THE KYRIAKOS VIRGIN BRIDE
#1822

BY TESSA RADLEY

Zac Kyriakos was in search of a woman pure both
in body and heart to marry, and he believed that Pandora
Armstrong was the answer to his prayers. When Pandora
discovered that Zac's true reason for marrying her was
because she was a virgin, she wanted an annulment. Little
did she know that Zac was beginning to fall in love with
her and would do anything not to let her go....

On sale September 2007 from Silhouette Desire.

BILLIONAIRE HEIRS:
They are worth a fortune...but can they be tamed?

Also look for
THE APOLLONIDIES MISTRESS SCANDAL
on sale October 2007
THE DESERT BRIDE OF AL SAYED
on sale November 2007

Available wherever books are sold.

COMING NEXT MONTH

**#1819 MILLIONAIRE'S WEDDING REVENGE—
Anna DePalo**
The Garrisons
This millionaire is determined to lure his ex-love back into his bed. Can she survive his game of seduction?

#1820 SEDUCED BY THE RICH MAN—Maureen Child
Reasons for Revenge
A business arrangement turns into a torrid affair when a mogul bribes a beautiful stranger into posing as his wife.

**#1821 THE BILLIONAIRE'S BABY NEGOTIATION—
Day Leclaire**
When the woman a billionaire sets out to seduce becomes pregnant, his plan to win control of her ranch isn't the only thing he'll be negotiating.

#1822 THE KYRIAKOS VIRGIN BRIDE—Tessa Radley
Billionaire Heirs
He must marry a virgin. She's the perfect choice. But his new bride's secret unleashes a scandal that rocks more than their marriage bed!

**#1823 THE MILLIONAIRE'S MIRACLE—
Cathleen Galitz**
She needed her ex-husband's help to fulfill her father's last wish. But will a night with the millionaire produce a miracle?

#1824 FORGOTTEN MARRIAGE—Paula Roe
He'd lost his memory of their time together. How could she welcome back her husband when he'd forgotten their tumultuous marriage?

SDCNM0807